A Time in the Sun

By
James E. Crowder

PublishAmerica
Baltimore

© 2008 by James E. Crowder.
All rights reserved. No part of this book may be reproduced, stored in a retrieval system or transmitted in any form or by any means without the prior written permission of the publishers, except by a reviewer who may quote brief passages in a review to be printed in a newspaper, magazine or journal.

First printing

All characters in this book are fictitious, and any resemblance to real persons, living or dead, is coincidental.

PublishAmerica has allowed this work to remain exactly as the author intended, verbatim, without editorial input.

ISBN: 1-60610-003-3
PUBLISHED BY PUBLISHAMERICA, LLLP
www.publishamerica.com
Baltimore

Printed in the United States of America

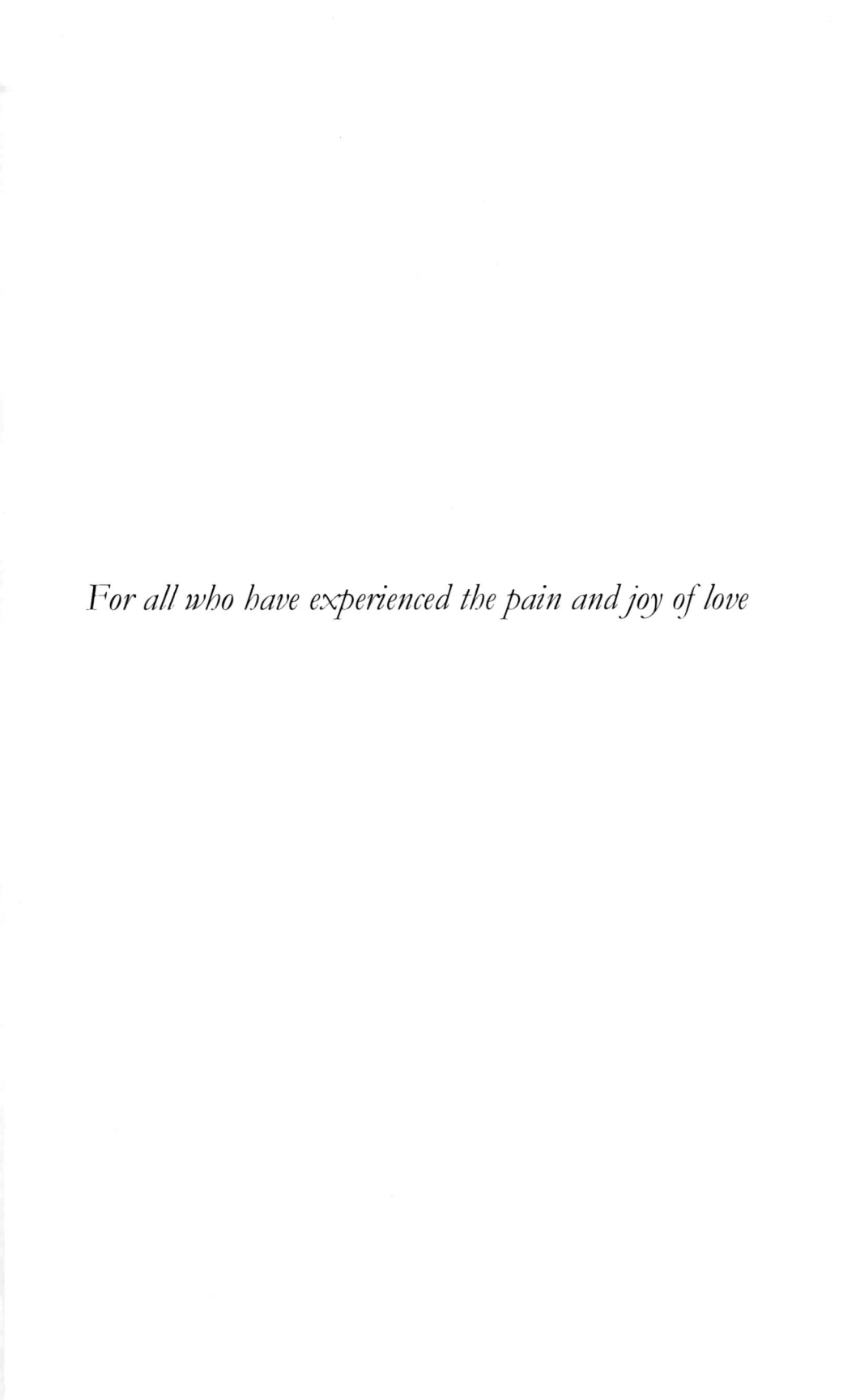

For all who have experienced the pain and joy of love

A Time in the Sun

Chapter One

Traveling alone through the universe in a small spacecraft, Patten gradually became aware that the glowing sun ahead was becoming larger, as Earth behind him grew smaller. Suspecting that his craft had become entangled in the gravitational pull of the sun, he switched on the port side thrusters to veer away. But too late! The thrusters were too weak to overcome the gravitational field of the sun.

The broiling mass of red, yellow and orange, loomed larger and larger ahead. He hurriedly switched on reverse thrusters to try and counter the sun's gravity, but to no avail. The craft flew faster and faster toward the sun! He tried frantically to escape by turning boosters on and off, but eventually recognized that he was trapped—there was no escape. His face burned from the sun's searing heat now permeating the craft's interior, and sweat ran down his face and clouded the visor of his helmet. Yet he could do nothing but ride the craft: he was helpless, a prisoner of the sun. He saw himself being drawn into and quickly incinerated in the ball of fire.

But just when all hope seemed lost, his spacecraft closely missed the fiery sphere and was unexpectedly propelled out into the solar system by the great momentum that had been created by the sun's gravitational pull. His moment of optimism quickly vanished, though, when he caught a glimpse of ice-covered objects, glinting in the rays of the sun, tumbling towards him. As the objects grew closer, he made them out to be…yes…two *metal caskets, one the size for a small child, the other larger, both now slowly rolling around his spacecraft. The caskets moved steadily closer, and to his horror he saw pictures stuck in the ice on top of the caskets. He squeezed his eyes shut...he didn't want to recognize...and when he opened his eyes again he found he had no control over the flight of the craft: it was helplessly flung out into the nothingness of space. As he saw Earth becoming only a speck behind him, in terror he realized he would be everlastingly unable to return to Earth—he would have no control over his destiny and would forever be estranged.*

Heart pounding, Patten thrashed about in a sweat, gradually awakening to the reality of his bedroom. He sat up in bed, his heart rate slowly returning to normal as he became fully aware of the here and now.

He hadn't slept well during the night, but seeing the time, he dutifully arose to shower and prepare to drive to the airport. Before he left the duplex, he telephoned for a weather briefing. The Jacksonville Flight Service Station reported a ceiling of 3,500 feet with 5 miles visibility; it was within the FAA's visual flight rules legal limits for private pilot flight instruction he had planned for the day. Weather conditions were forecast to deteriorate during the afternoon.

Patten had been dreading to see this day come for more than a month, and prepared for it by planning a full day of flight instruction, taking students back to back to hopefully keep his mind occupied and off disturbing thoughts and memories. Flying required concentration— teaching flying required more concentration. He knew that, while keeping the mind busy by performing well-practiced procedures automatically during an in-flight emergency may not solve the urgent situation, it does prevent panic; would the same held true of personal emergencies, he wondered.

Skipping breakfast, he drove to Gulf Shores Aviation oblivious to his surroundings, except for once swerving to dodge crows feeding on carrion in the road, an amorphous mass of blood and flesh. The protruding ringed tail identified it as an armadillo.

The air was heavy with suffocating humidity, and the sky was overcast with gloomy, dark, low stratus clouds when Patten arrived at the small airport near the resort city of Gulf Shores on the Alabama coast. On this morning, the airport had a look of unreality: the weak light filtering through the low clouds imbued the facilities and airplanes with an eerie pallor.

Patten was anxious to become engrossed in work, and was relieved when he saw that his first student of the day had arrived and was preflighting one of the two-seat trainers, a Cessna one fifty-two. He fell into his work and forced himself to concentrate on flying and instructing.

By two o'clock light rain was falling and visibility had diminished to less than three miles—not enough for flight under VFR or visual flight rules, including private pilot flight training. Patten was not disappointed, because he had reached the point that he could not focus on flight training as well as he knew he should. He climbed out of the Cessna trainer with John Tidwell, a lanky twenty-one year old private pilot student. Searching the ramp, Patten found a set of yellow chocks to cradle the nose wheel of the Cessna; light airplanes were susceptible to being blown around if they weren't chocked or tied down, as there was always a breeze on the Gulf.

As they walked through sprinkling rain across the ramp toward the flight instruction offices, John handed his logbook to Patten for endorsement and recording of the lesson. "When do you think I'll be ready to solo?" asked John eagerly.

Patten's 180-pound, 6-foot body felt heavy, as though he carried a 300-pound backpack. He was short of breath and struggled to walk the short distance to the office, although he regularly jogged and was in good physical condition for a forty-five year old. He made an effort to gather his thoughts: "Probably a couple more lessons. We'll have to work out some minor problems in the traffic pattern," Patten replied.

John tended to demand immediate perfection and was in a hurry to finish his flight training. "How about flying again Sunday afternoon?"

Patten thought for a moment. "The morning will be better for me. I have banners to pull Sunday afternoon. Do you want to put the next lesson off until the following Saturday?"

"Oh, I can't be here Sunday morning, and I don't want to get rusty!" John replied, frustrated. "I'm anxious to solo."

Patten sighed and relented: "Okay. See if Linda can move my schedule around to find a spot for you in the next few days."

Patten opened the door and followed the student into the lobby of Gulf Shores Aviation, an airport business referred to by the FAA as an FBO, or fixed base operator, a designation of old that had little to do with current aviation reality. Pictures of classic and new airplanes decorated the walls, and large posters of cockpits hung behind the counter.

A slender, bleached blonde with short hair, attractive figure, and wearing much makeup to cover harsh facial features, looked up as they walked in. Linda wore gaudy costume jewelry, a blatantly revealing low-plunging blouse, tight-fitting jeans and high heels. She was 25 years old, and had just gone through her fourth husband.

Patten made an entry for the lesson into John's logbook, and then turned to Linda. "Please cancel the other students scheduled for this afternoon since the weather is below minimums. Reschedule them for next week. And fit John in as soon as possible."

"Okay, but don't run off," she said as she handed him a clipboard with a student application. "A new student is waiting for you in the pilot's lounge."

Oh God, I don't think I can talk to another person today. Not on this day! He had held together for about as long as he could, but was near the breaking point. Being absorbed in flight instruction had allowed him to suppress dark thoughts that were now clamoring for attention as his mental and physical fatigue lowered his resistance.

He sighed heavily: "Is it my turn to take a new student?" There were three other flight instructors in the flight-training program.

"Yeah, you're up!" said Linda, "Not only that," she added, "the woman asked for the oldest flight instructor here, the one with the most experience, and I think that's you. Scared out of her wits, I think. But you're the boss," she whined as she worked on a mouthful of gum. "Do you want me to have another flight instructor take her? Ralph is out on the ramp," she offered, more helpful than usual.

"It's my turn, I'll take her," Patten grunted.

Linda lowered her voice and wrinkled her nose. "I warn you, she doesn't look like much—not what you'd call 'hot'!"

Patten left John and Linda at the counter, and dragged himself toward the pilots' lounge. He entered the open door of the lounge, a small room containing a television, table with flight plan forms, and telephone used to contact the flight service station to obtain weather reports and file flight plans. The room was filled with soft leather furniture and the seemingly essential feature of every pilots' lounge, the omnipresent coffee maker.

A female figure sat huddled on the edge of the couch, nervously leafing through a magazine while obviously paying no attention to its content. The new student was in her late twenties, of medium height with black hair, and appeared carelessly and casually dressed in baggy jeans and blouse. She wore no makeup and had paid scant attention to her hair. There was a splash of color in her dress—a red scarf tied loosely about her neck—that contrasted sharply with her generally drab appearance.

Patten struggled with the heaviness pressing on his shoulders. An image of two caskets flashed through his mind. *Steve died five years ago. He was fourteen at the time. How would he have looked, what would he have been like, at the age of nineteen?* He shook his head to clear his mind, to come out of the dream-like state.

*She's speaking…listen….she's talking…*Patten forced his attention, as through a fog, back into the present. He saw the new student sitting across from him, although he didn't remember sitting down. She was asking in a weak and querulous voice if he was the person who taught flying, Patten surmised.

December 21. I hate this day. I hate all anniversaries: birthdays, weddings, holidays and deaths. When will the pain ever stop? Or will it ever stop? Every year seems as bad as the last.

"I…I'm Patten Fortis, one of the flight instructors here. I understand that you want to learn to fly."

"Yes," she said, anxiety mixed with an undercurrent of determination in her voice. "I'm scared, but I would like to try."

Patten mustered all his strength to concentrate and was eventually able to access the correct memory file. He spoke in a monotone with computer-like precision: "Everyone is afraid at first, but everyone seems to get over it. You'll be all right. We won't go any faster than you feel able, and I won't do anything to scare you," he said. He went on to repeat correctly and clinically the requirements to earn a private pilot's license: A minimum of twenty hours of dual instruction and twenty hours of supervised solo instruction, the successful completion of a written test on rules, regulations, and procedures of flying, weather, responsibilities of a pilot, and so forth, information that would be covered very well in ground school that she was expected to attend two nights a week for six weeks. She would have to obtain a medical certificate before she soloed, or flew alone, and would have to take and pass a short written test before the first solo. To finally obtain the private pilot license she would need to pass a flight test conducted by an FAA examiner after she completed her training and was signed off by her flight instructor to take the test. She would have many opportunities to take sample written tests and to practice performing flight procedures required by FAA examiners until she was proficient enough to pass the test. She was reassured that all of this information would be repeated in the first ground school class and that she would have ample time to ask questions about the requirements then.

Patten was in a hurry to leave. "Any questions?" he asked, suspecting that she had heard more than she was interested in hearing, and certainly more than she was likely to remember.

"No..." she said, and then with wide eyes she blurted: "But I think you don't understand—I'm very scared, terrified! The thing I'm most interested in is conquering my fear. I've always been a fearful person, and I'm most afraid of flying, even as a passenger. I flew on an airline once and had a panic attack. I thought I was going to die! I've never been on an airplane since.

"It's so embarrassing. I even get dizzy at small heights, like standing on chairs! Do you know what I mean? Do you think I can do it?"

Compassion for the new student's apprehension brought Patten more firmly, albeit only momentarily, into the present. "I think that will be less of a problem than you suppose, uh..." he glanced at the application sheet, "Mrs. Price. And—"

"Call me Carley," she interrupted.

"I was going to say," he continued, "an interesting thing is that people who're afraid of heights are often not afraid of heights as long as they are enclosed, such as in the cockpit of an airplane. And, some people who are afraid to fly find their fear subsides when they learn to control the airplane. Maybe that will be your reaction. But regardless, you took the first step to face your fear, and if you can hang on for five or six lessons, I think your fear will go away. I don't remember having any students here that didn't lose their fear after a few lessons."

He began to feel a fraud. The urge to leave mounted. To seem so confident on the outside while barely holding together on the inside made him feel unstable, adrift, and an imposter. The walls were closing in. "I have to go now," he said. "We'll have your first flight lesson on Saturday if that's okay with you. If not, work out a day with Linda, the receptionist, that's convenient for you. I usually give flight instruction to new students in the mornings because the air is smoother then."

"Any morning but Wednesdays is okay with me," she quickly said, slightly more confidently. "So Saturday is good. But can you tell me more about the training? I think I will relax more if I know what to expect. Do you know what I mean?" she asked plaintively.

"I have to go. Just have Linda set it up, then. She'll have some materials for you to look over, and I'll tell you more about it the next time we meet."

He hurriedly left the new student and exited the offices through the back door. He crossed the ramp past a one eighty-five Skywagon, an airplane that today appeared especially awkward and out of place tied down on the ramp, as it stood high on small wheels hidden under large amphibian floats. He drove away from the two buildings that comprised the offices and maintenance hangar of Gulf Shores Aviation. Turning south on Highway 59, he stopped at Delchamps to pick up a six-pack of beer. He thought a drink might perk him up.

Returning to the car he drove south again and turned right on

Windmill Ridge Road to the duplex he rented—a weathered, rustic-looking building supported by high pilings for protection from flooding during hurricanes. The building looked drearier and more precariously balanced than usual. He had an image of the whole structure swaying and tumbling off the pilings. Once inside, he opened a beer and put the remainder of the six-pack inside the refrigerator. While sitting on the couch sipping beer, he flipped on the television. Emptiness…a void…crept from his stomach to his chest. He stared at the television but didn't see it; he drank the beer from his trembling hand but didn't taste it.

Numbers began running through his mind, as they had for the past few weeks. He remembered, when it first happened, he was driving along the highway, and noticed that he was counting the centerline stripes. Feeling foolish, he tried to stop, but couldn't. If he stopped counting, panic overcame him.

He had begun, also, to take a great interest in numbers. Tortuous calculations became a pressing concern. He would sometimes feel compelled to log the miles he drove, the gallons of fuel he purchased, and would then calculate the miles per gallon. He figured the cost per mile. He also computed the cost per mile of flying the training airplane, taking into account projected maintenance costs, annual insurance divided by the number of hours he judged the airplane would fly in a full year, avionics maintenance, fuel, oil, and depreciation of engine and airframe. Special anxiety came with the ambiguity of certain costs, and he would spend hours trying to work out an acceptable formula for determining the exact cost of repairs. He was puzzled, because he knew, on the one hand, that all of this was ridiculous, but on the other hand, he was unable to stop.

A sense of impending doom slowly came upon him. He fought the urge to run out of the duplex. He'd made a barbershop appointment for 4:30, and somehow welcomed the obligation.

As the time for the appointment drew near, Patten left the duplex but was gripped by nervousness as he descended the steps to the street, worrying that the whole structure would collapse at any moment. Rain fell steadily, and cracking thunder in the distance signaled the proximity of storm clouds.

As he drove along the beach to the barbershop through hard showers, he had lapses of concentration. At times he wondered if he had stopped at a traffic light along the way. Occasionally, he was brought to himself by bursts of thunder. He felt fortunate when he reached the barbershop without smashing into anyone.

The barber, a heavy man in his early sixties with a patchy short beard, kept up his usual continuous one-way conversation about Alabama football as he trimmed Patten's gray-speckled black hair. The barber wore his ego on the shoulders of the football team, and his mood rose and fell with the team's fortunes each year.

Patten became increasingly anxious when the barber picked up a straight razor. He began to worry that he could not hold his head still when the barber shaved around his hairline. Images of the sharp razor cutting into his eyes flashed into his mind and horrified him, and he struggled to obliterate the images. He became so concerned that he used his utmost strength to keep his head from shaking, yet the more he tried, the more he shook. He wanted to leap out of the chair and race out the door.

The barber continued his musing about the current problems with Alabama football, ignorant of the conflict taking place in the barber chair. He reached for the straight razor and began scraping along Patten's right ear. The barber abruptly stopped talking in the middle of a sentence because Patten's head suddenly jerked to the left. The man stepped back and saw that the razor had sliced the upper part of Patten's right ear and the scalp above the ear. The barber grabbed a towel and held it against the cut.

"Son, you almost lost an ear!" he said to Patten, puzzled "Why did you move your head like that?"

"It's okay, it's my fault," Patten stammered, too panicked to be embarrassed, "I have to go now!" Patten jumped from the chair, pulled the apron over his head, left a twenty-dollar bill on the counter and rushed out the door.

The razor was too sharp to cause any immediate pain, but Patten felt the warm trickle of blood running down his ear and along his neck as he ran to his car and drove off. He wanted to go to his apartment and hide. He didn't bother to catch the blood oozing down his neck as he hurried along the coastal highway. *Highway 59. Fifty-nine highways, half are 29.5 running north and south. Gulf Shores is about 25% or maybe 20%, or 15% of the difference of the east to the west coast. Fifty-nine is 15% of what number? No, 29.5 is 15% of what number?*

The siren and flashing light alongside his car brought him out of his reverie. The highway patrol car was five feet from his face. The patrolman was motioning angrily for Patten to pull over. Parking at the side of the road with the patrol car behind him, Patten was shaking when the patrolman walked up to his window.

The patrolman's voice sounded far off and strange to Patten. The voice had a hollow ring to it, as though it were coming to him through a metal pipe. "Man, what's wrong with you? I've been behind you for a mile with my siren on and lights flashing! You blind?" The officer spied the blood on Patten's neck. "Man, you all right?"

"Damn the...okay. Just a little cut, an accident. What did I do wrong, why'd you stop me?"

"You ran a stop sign back there. You didn't even slow down. You could have killed someone. Give me your license." The officer sniffed and looked around in Patten's car.

After taking Patten's driver's license, the officer walked back to the patrol car. Shortly the officer returned and was writing on a pad he tried to shield from the light rain. "Everything seems to be in order. I'm going to give you a ticket for running a stop sign, fellow, but you're in no shape to drive. Bring your keys, lock your car, and come with me."

"But officer, I'm okay," Patten protested. "I really am. I just had something on my mind."

The officer was insistent: "Listen, buddy, I'm going to do you a favor. I don't know what's wrong with you. Maybe you're a drug freak, I don't know. And then I don't know where you got that nasty cut. I'm taking you to the hospital emergency room and will leave you there. You can pick up your car later. You don't belong on the road—you're going to kill somebody, or yourself!"

The officer drove Patten to the county hospital, and took him into the ER lobby. He placed Patten in line for the receptionist desk and left. The police escort had brought special attention from the ER patients to Patten, whose anxiety was rising again as the patients stared at him.

In the lobby of the emergency room patients lined the walls, some standing and some sitting. Lying on the floor, a man gasped for breath while a woman held a blood-soaked cloth against his throat. Patten felt queasiness at the sight, and spasms of nausea began churning up from his stomach.

The receptionist was cool and aloof. She spoke in an even tone to the agitated man leaning over her desk—a man covered with dirt, sweat and blood. "Sir," she was saying, "we will get to your brother as soon as we can. First, I need some information." She stared at the man in front of her, waiting for some sign of cooperation.

The man was irate. "I can't believe that a person comes in here bleeding to death from a chainsaw cut, and all you want to do is get his full name, address, and social security number—"

The receptionist, interrupting, was unperturbed: "Yes sir, and health insurance number, employer and that of—"

"Listen, damn it, my brother is dying…"

Patten ran into the men's room, opened a stall and heaved into the commode. The vomit burned his mouth and throat and choked him. The rancid odor added to his nausea.

Going to the sink, he splashed cold water on his face and dried off with paper towels. Back in the stall, he flushed the toilet. The toilet stuck on flush. The loud rushing, boiling sound from the industrial toilet reverberated on the tiled floor and walls, growing louder and louder until the roaring, hollow sound reached a crescendo that drove him running out of the restroom, out the door and down the street.

Patten ran through a driving rain until he was breathless and soaked. Suddenly realizing that he must look bizarre running down the street with blood on the side of his head and on his shirt, he slowed to a fast walk to avoid attracting attention. Stopping at the first telephone booth he came across, he called a taxi, retrieved his automobile, and returned to his duplex.

He felt exhausted when the anxiety wore off, and he fell into a deep depression. He had the presence of mind to call Linda to tell her that he would not be in the next day and to cancel everything he had on the books. She asked what to do about a charter flight scheduled for the next evening. He asked if she would call another flight instructor to take it, and he then took the telephone off the hook.

He collapsed on the couch, unconcerned about his wet, bloodied and soiled clothes. *I must be going crazy…schizophrenia, maybe.*

Chapter Two

He awoke early the next morning in a state of despair. Deciding his condition, whatever it was, was not getting any better, he undressed, showered, then looked through the yellow pages and found the number of a clinical psychologist. Dr. Copeland's office was a few miles away in Fairhope on Mobile Bay. He told the receptionist that he needed to be seen as soon as possible, and was given an appointment at eleven o'clock.

Not feeling at all hungry, Patten drove over to the small town of Fairhope and ferreted out Dr. Copeland's offices. His heart raced as he entered the building, and then slowed as he became engrossed in counting the steps down the main hallway. Opening the door to Copeland's offices, he made his way into the lobby, completed an information sheet provided by the receptionist, and to have something to do to relieve his anxiety, helped himself to a cup of coffee provided for patients in the lobby. He nervously sat down in the lobby to wait.

From an interior hallway a lobby door soon opened, and toward Patten walked a casually dressed, slightly heavy and bearded man with bushy eyebrows. The man appeared to walk toward him through a tunnel.

He perused Patten's information sheet, eyed him over carefully, and then spoke.

The psychologist's voice sounded as an echo. "I'm Glen Copeland," he said in a calm and unhurried voice as he offered a hand to Patten.

Patten stood, but in doing so bumped his coffee cup with his arm and knocked it to the floor. He quickly picked up the cup. But his trembling hands fumbled it again.

The receptionist rushed over. "I'll take care of this," she said.

Dr. Copeland smiled, "Accidents happen, and sometimes at the worst of times."

They shook hands. Patten could feel his own hand as cold and clammy in Dr. Copeland's strong and warm hand. "Please come with me," said the psychologist, as he limped slowly toward the lobby door. Patten began to feel more relaxed as he followed Dr. Copeland into an inner hall.

The psychologist limped down the hallway and entered an office with Patten close behind. He closed the office door and motioned for Patten to sit on a leather chair before his desk. Dragging his right leg behind the desk, Copeland sat down and, after looking at Patten for a minute, peered out the slits of the blind-covered window.

"Kind of nerve-wracking to see a psychologist for the first time, huh?"

"Yes. But I...I guess I'm going crazy! I don't know what's happening to me! And it's getting worse! I go from panic to depression, nothing in between," Patten said, gloomily. "I've tried to deal with this, but it's getting worse."

"That bad, huh?" Dr. Copeland chuckled.

Patten didn't see anything funny. He described what had happened the day before. The hollow, loud and unrelenting sound of the flushing toilet still stuck in his head. When he finished relating the experience, he waited a moment then glanced at the psychologist who seemed relaxed.

"I don't know. I guess I'm coming apart," he said, uncertainly and weakly. "I hope you can help me."

Dr. Copeland gazed with kind blue eyes at Patten, who quickly looked away. He then said, in a measured voice, "I think we'll find that you have all the answers, Mr. Fortis."

"Well, what about the counting…the obsessions…? Isn't that crazy?"

"Seems a good way to keep your mind occupied. I suggest we don't worry about that right now. I have a feeling the counting will go away on its own."

Patten relented. "Well, okay, but I thought I would need some psychoactive medication."

"That's one way to handle it. I think we'll move along faster, though, if we can understand what's happening. Medication might blunt your feelings and in that way give you a little quick relief but take away some of your sensitivity. And, you're a pilot and flight instructor, as you indicated on the information sheet. I suspect that piloting airplanes while taking psychotropic medications is not recommended or allowed. Is that right?"

"Yes," Patten said. "That's right, of course."

"Your anxieties, uncomfortable though they are, will help us to understand what's going on with you," he said. He paused for a minute, and then continued: "I guess you've been struggling a long time with anxiety and depression."

Patten realized that he had always been tormented by fear, a kind of apprehensive dread that, of late years, had been gripping him relentlessly, worse lately. He could not remember a time when he had not been dreading something. When he was a little boy it was always there—everywhere—the fear. There had always been the ominous "something" in a corner of his mind, the dark place in which he dared not look, yet from which he could at any moment be attacked. Maybe if he did not seem a threat…

"I suppose you've thought about ending it all?"

In a flash Patten remembered dropping a marking flag from a Cessna Agwagon at the end of a run at the edge of a cotton field in Texas, and then clipping a telephone line with the right wing. The cutting wire that stretched from the fuselage to the top of the tail sliced through two power lines. A third line hung on the tail and the Agwagon stalled and flat-spun sideways to the ground. The wheels and propeller were violently separated from the airplane, but the reinforced fuselage held together. Bruised and awash with insecticide, he kicked out a window and crawled away from the wreck. He didn't feel frightened. In fact, he remembered feeling a little disappointed, or even depressed. He didn't understand it then. Maybe he wanted to die. Maybe he knew the power lines were there; he must have seen them when he scouted the field before the flight.

"You were thinking…"

"Well, anyway, I would not consciously try to take my own life. I would feel such a complete failure."

Copeland was silent for a moment. "I suppose you've been struggling with some strong, unpleasant feelings for a long time."

"That's true. But things are generally going better now, at least on the surface," Patten reflected. "The business I have seems to be growing. I did go through some unhappy times a few years ago…I guess I never really dealt with them well, and still don't. I don't like to think about them.

"I try to control those thoughts—unpleasant thoughts—and unpleasant memories. I try to avoid the unpleasantness and stay away from things that upset me. Doesn't work sometimes, I guess."

The psychologist chuckled. "Seems the harder you try to control thoughts, the more they go out of control. A professor I once had used to demonstrate to the class the futility of trying to control thoughts by asking everyone to try not to think of the most vulgar word they'd ever heard."

"Oh, I see you're right…but just thinking about them is upsetting, doesn't help!"

After a long while, Patten sighed and stared at the floor sheepishly. "Well, it's a long story, as they say, and I don't want to bore you, but I guess you need to know my past to understand my situation."

Copeland gazed out the window, but was attentive. "I'm interested in whatever you want to tell me."

Patten took a deep breath, and in anguish related the tragedies he lived through a few years past, a short time before he went into aviation.

He fought to control the tears, but they trickled down his face as he related the tragic circumstances of his past. Embarrassed by the tears, he struggled to recover control. The psychologist handed him tissues.

"I'm sorry," he said, as he took the tissues and wiped his eyes.

"You've been through a great deal."

"I'd had some interest in aviation since childhood, so I took the $150,000 that was my part of the divorce settlement, and paid for training as a private pilot, commercial pilot, took instrument training, and then additional training at a school in Georgia to spread fertilize, herbicide and insecticide by air.

"Aerial application is a very solitary job," said he. "The only thing I could handle at the time, I thought. I'd made a mess of my life. I didn't want any friends, wanted to stay away from people—didn't feel up to dealing with anything besides work. But I tired quickly of the chemical smell always present in the cockpit, on my clothes and on me, and dry West Texas where I first worked. I then went to an accelerated flight school in Florida for multiengine, flight instructor, and ATP—airline transport pilot—training and hired out at an operation in Panama City as a flight instructor, charter pilot and pilot towing advertising banners. I moved here a little over a year ago and started a small school of flight instruction, and to make ends meet I tow advertising banners and fly charter flights out of Gulf Shores Aviation.

"I blocked the past out of my mind, as much as I could, but these…I guess I have this…uh…. reaction around this time of the year, when my life starts coming apart. Holidays are terrible, for some reason: I turn into a basket case. I try not to think about it. But the bad feelings seem to get worse every year, instead of better."

"I see."

A short silence followed.

"Anything else you wish to tell me today?" Dr. Copeland asked, softly.

"No, that's about it. Do you have any questions for me?"

"You're doing fine. If you'd like, we'll get together again next week to work on the problems that are bothering you." He jotted down some notes in a folder.

"I'd like to. I can't go on this way."

"I see you have a rather unusual first name, Mr. Fortis."

"Yes. Unusual spelling…the story I heard is that my father admired General Patton of WWII fame, and wanted to name me 'Patton.' My mother wanted to name me 'Thomas,' after an uncle. Dad won out, but my mother misspelled my name on the birth certificate. My dad, as the story goes, was furious, and he never let mom forget how stupid he thought she was. Mother never apologized for the error. I've had to live with it, and went through elementary school, high school, and even college correcting teachers to spell my name with an 'en' instead of an 'on.'"

Dr. Copeland grinned, "Maybe your mother *wasn't* stupid, after all."

"What?"

"Your mother had her methods, I suppose, to get what she wanted, or to punish others when she didn't." Copeland arose, limped to the door and opened it for Patten. He shook Patten's hand. "Have Ruth to reschedule you for next week," he said as he handed the chart to Patten.

"Thanks," said Patten. "I feel better, but I'm afraid I've depressed you with all my problems."

Copeland chuckled: "I get paid for listening to problems. Look forward to seeing you next week!"

After making another appointment, Patten left Fairhope for Gulf Shores feeling emotionally drained but somehow more relaxed than he had been in months.

That night he was visited by a strange dream: He and his father are in a cinder block building with a concrete floor. Patten has a neurological problem that causes him to suddenly lose consciousness and collapse, then quickly regain consciousness and control of his muscles.

His father, who looked old and feeble, grabbed at him as he started falling. Patten didn't want his father to try and catch him for fear his father would fall and hurt himself. But Patten fell, his father *did* try to catch him, and they both tumbled to the floor. Patten then noticed his mother was standing in the doorway, contentedly watching.

When Patten regained his footing, he explained to his father: "I sometimes have syncopal episodes and fall down. When I start to fall, don't try and catch me. I'll be okay. In a short time I'll be able to get back up on my own."

Chapter Three

A few days later Patten arrived at the airport at nine o'clock and met with John Tidwell. He and John practiced take off and landings to prepare John for solo flight.

At ten o'clock, Carley appeared at the airport for her first lesson. She was dressed without make up and her face was ashen; the paleness stood out in sharp contrast with her bright blue eyes and shoulder-length dark hair. Patten felt a vague uneasiness around her.

He recalled that she was very nervous about flying, and today, her anxiety was clearly telegraphed in her wide eyes, trembling hands, and occasional quiver in her voice. Patten's attention was drawn away from his thoughts by the fear he saw in her. He began to feel compassion for this new student, compassion that again pushed his own worries to the back of his mind. He also admired her. *She's gutsy to be here, thinking this will be the last day of her life.*

He planned the first lesson to be a confidence builder: she needed to learn that the airplane would not unexpectedly drop out of the sky. "Let's not worry a lot about learning how to fly today," he said. "Let's just take an airplane ride and see what flying is all about." He tried to seem upbeat and unconcerned.

He performed a preflight inspection on the Cessna trainer, explaining the what and why of each procedure. "You'll take the pilot's seat, the left seat," he said, as he opened the portside door for her. He helped her with the seatbelt and shoulder harness, and then removed the chocks from the nose wheel. Climbing in beside her, he was acutely aware of their bodies touching. The one fifty-two cockpit was crowded, even with Patten's tall and slender 180 pounds and Carley's petite frame. He felt uncomfortable. "These trainer cockpits are small," he apologized.

He gave her a headphone set. "This is likely to mess up your hair," he managed a slight smile.

"I...think it looks so bad nothing could hurt it," she laughed nervously.

Patten showed her how to adjust the microphone, and he toggled the master switch to ensure they could hear each other. Finding that the headsets worked adequately, he quickly completed the pre-start checklist, started the one fifty-two, and taxied to the runway while getting a radio check.

He explained in detail what he was doing in order to build her confidence in him and in the airplane, although he expected she would remember very little about this first flight. Explaining each procedure, he performed the run up: setting the flight instruments, checking magnetos, carburetor heat, and flight controls, and told her what to anticipate at lift off. He told her he would always explain what they were going to do before they did it, and that he would never intentionally surprise nor try to scare her. She nodded understanding, and appeared to relax a bit.

"We'll take off towards the south, then turn back north, climb to 3,000 feet and just fly around."

Guiding the one fifty-two out onto the centerline of the runway, Patten pushed the throttle firmly all the way forward and started down the runway. At 55 knots, he applied back pressure to the yoke, and allowed the airplane to fly itself completely off the runway.

He glanced at the new student: she had lost all of the little color she had and her knuckles were white as she grasped the yoke tightly as though she might fall. "Are we flying!?" she blurted out.

"We are," he grinned, "and this is the first of many flights for you."

Seeing that she was trying to keep herself vertical as he banked the airplane to the west, he said: "Everybody does that at first. Relax as much as you can, roll with the airplane, and you'll find that you'll be comfortable and won't get tired."

"The houses and cars look so much smaller from up here, don't they?" she asked, excitedly.

Patten nodded, pleased that the new student had allowed herself to look out the window at the objects below. He leveled off at 3,000 feet and pulled power back to cruise. "Mrs. Price…Carley…," he said, "this airplane has a ten to one glide ratio at the best glide airspeed, which is 60 knots. It's a very reliable airplane, but if the engine should ever fail, we would not fall straight down out of the sky. The 'ten to one glide ratio' means that if the engine should quit and we could not get it restarted, we can set up the proper airspeed and glide ten feet forward for every one foot we lose in altitude. If we were flying a mile high, for instance, we would be able to glide for ten miles before we reached the ground, which is plenty of time and distance to reach a runway or landing spot off the airport property.

"I'm not going to shut the engine down, but I'm going to pull the power back to idle and show you what I mean. I know you'll be nervous, naturally, but you'll see that things will go our way."

He pulled the throttle back and turned on the carburetor heat. The engine slowed to idle, and the airspeed dropped back as Patten held the altitude by putting back pressure on the yoke. When the airspeed fell to 60 knots, he held the airspeed constant by beginning a slow descent. "See, the airplane doesn't fall." He glanced over at her for her reaction, but she didn't look all that impressed.

"We'll make a shallow bank. Look at all of that flat land down there, plenty of places to park this little airplane. And we would have almost enough time to read *War and Peace* before we got there."

She laughed, "Okay, you made your point, but I know *that's* an exaggeration!"

Patten laughed, too, the first time in a long time, he thought. "Okay, I stretched it a bit."

Removing the carburetor heat at 1,000 feet, he added power, and climbed back to 3,000 feet. He had Carley practice using the controls. She learned to use the ailerons to bank and the rudder to turn. Although the slipping turns made Patten a little nauseated, he knew that coordination of the rudder and ailerons did not take students very long to learn. "You're doing fine," he said.

Sensing that she was tiring, he took over again and returned to the airport.

On final approach, Carley asked: "What does the 'eighteen' mean, those large numbers painted on the runway?"

"Oh," Patten couldn't suppress a slight grin, "pilots call that 'one-eight.' Runways are numbered according to magnetic courses. The zero is dropped. 'One-eight' means that the magnetic course of this runway is around one hundred and eighty degrees. Runway seven is actually seven zero; two seven is west, or two hundred and seventy degrees. We'll almost always take off and land here at Gulf Shores Aviation on runway one-eight, because the wind usually blows from the Gulf. You'll learn these things in ground school and in your books."

Carley nodded understanding.

He set the one fifty-two down on one-eight. Full color had returned to the new student's face, and she was smiling. *She's probably relieved and surprised that she has not met her death on this flight.*

"Wow, that was fun!" she exclaimed.

"It was," he agreed, "but there is some drudgery to learning to fly. When we get into the office, you'll have some lessons to pick up. We'll schedule you for ground school and your next flying lesson."

"Okay. I'm looking forward to it!" she smiled.

After the airplane was secured, they walked silently across the ramp to the flight instruction room. While he recorded the lesson in her logbook, Carley inspected the room. "Why are these pieces of shirts hanging on the wall?" she asked.

"Oh, those are shirttails of students. When a student completes the first solo, the back of his or her shirt is cut off. The event is recorded and authenticated on the shirttail by the flight instructor. The shirttail is then tacked to the wall here. It's a tradition for flight instructors to cut the shirttail off the student after the first solo flight, and on it to write the student's name, date of the solo, N-number of the aircraft, and name of the instructor. Most of the instructors these days have students to bring in an old shirt—not a $120 new shirt—before the solo flight. Most of the instructors perform some artwork on the shirt: something characteristic and perhaps unique about the student's training. The whole thing amounts to an initiation into the world of airplane pilots and celebration of the student's accomplishment. Your shirttail will be up there in a few weeks," he said, confidently.

"If you say so…but I don't know. I can't really believe I'll be able to fly alone someday. I couldn't think beyond just starting flight instruction, before today, or just flying, for that matter, or just staying alive!" she said wistfully.

"You'll make it," he said as he handed the logbook back to her. "Would you have Linda reschedule us, give you your lesson plans, and set you up for ground school?" he asked quickly.

"Of course," she replied, initially confused by his sudden hurry but then attributing it to a heavy instruction schedule. "See you next time and thank you! Have a Merry Christmas!"

"Oh, yes. You too," he called after her as she left the room.

Chapter Four

Carley appeared early for her second flight lesson scheduled at ten o'clock the next week. Linda buzzed Patten on the intercom: "Your next student is here," she said, and then more quietly, "guess she can't tell time, huh?"

Patten didn't respond to the sarcasm. But it was only nine thirty, and he had paperwork to finish. "Tell her to wait in the pilot's lounge, and to read over her ground school notes."

"Yes sir!" Linda said, with exaggerated deference.

At ten o'clock sharp, Patten took Carley out of the pilot's lounge and they walked together out on the ramp to the Cessna one fifty-two. She was not nearly as fearful as she had been on the first flight.

A few fleecy, thin cumulus clouds dotted the blue sky. "It's a beautiful day," she said, scanning the sky.

"Yes, it is," Patten agreed, as he took notice. Then, anxious to get to work, "Today, I want you to preflight the airplane using a checklist. Always use the checklist, whether or not you have it memorized. The purpose of the preflight inspection is to determine whether the airplane is airworthy. I'll help you this time and again at our next lesson. After that, you'll be expected to do the preflight each time a few minutes before our lesson so that we'll have more time for flight."

A full twenty minutes was spent on the preflight. Carley was shown how to step up on the fuselage to check fuel in each tank in the wings, to open the cowling to see that the engine had enough oil, to check the air pressure impact and static openings and the stall warning apparatus, and what to look for while inspecting the ailerons, rudder and elevator. With practice, she would learn to finish the preflight inspection in five minutes.

Preflight completed, they entered the cockpit, belted themselves in and put on headphones. With Patten's help, Carley went through the pre-start checklist and after a couple of pumps on the primer and engaging the starter, the engine roared to life. He had her to warm the engine at 1,000 rpm on the tachometer, and had her check the oil pressure and switch on the strobe light.

"A couple of things before we start moving, Mrs. Price—"

"Carley," she reminded him.

"Sorry. First, I usually handle the radio for the first few lessons. And, second, we'll want to know who is in control of the airplane at all times. If you hear me say 'I've got it!' I'll want you to take your hands and feet off everything immediately, and I'll take control. Otherwise, you'll have control of the airplane. Okay?"

"Yes," she said tightly.

He called for a traffic advisory on the Unicom frequency, and with no traffic reported, announced his intentions for the benefit of other aircraft in the vicinity.

"On the ground, you guide the airplane with the rudder pedals. Push the left one, the nose wheel turns left; push the right one and the nose wheel turns right. Place your hands in your lap: you'll learn steering with your feet faster that way. Let's taxi to the runway, at about the speed of a fast walk."

She wobbled from side to side down the taxiway. At the run-up line just prior to entering the runway, Patten applied the toe brakes at the top of the rudder pedals to stop the airplane. Carley felt the brakes with her toes, and alternated putting the brakes on and off until she was satisfied she could stop the airplane safely on the ground.

Pulling out the take-off checklist from a pocket in the seatback rear, he explained the procedure to her as they completed each item. He taught her to throttle up to 1700 rpm, and to turn the switch key to check both right and left magnetos. He showed her how to check the carburetor heat. Finally, he had her set the flight instruments: the directional gyroscope to reflect the compass reading, and the attitude indicator to level on the artificial horizon.

Before taxiing onto the runway, he cautioned her to scan the runway and sky for any airplanes taking off or landing. On take off, Carley handled the power mostly, and Patten unobtrusively pushed on the rudder pedals to keep the airplane near the centerline of the runway, and pressed back on the yoke to get airborne after Carley did not respond with enough force as Patten gently kept suggesting, "back, back, back," as they barreled down the runway. The wings tottered back and forth, and the nose pitched up and down with Carley fighting to control the airplane as it bobbed its way into the air. She wasn't completely rattled, but beads of sweat broke out on her forehead. She was unaware of the help that Patten was giving with his fingers pressed against the bottom of the yoke on the right seat side and his feet lightly pushing on the rudder pedals; hence there was no actual danger of loss of control.

"That's fine for your first take off," he said. "I'll take over now and give you a rest. We'll climb to 3,000 feet and level off. Today we'll work on straight and level flight, banks, and turns to headings."

At 3,000, he leveled off and turned the trim tab until all pressure was off the yoke. He demonstrated how the airplane would stay at 3,000 feet, if properly trimmed, with his hands off the yoke, and how the horizon looked in relation to the windscreen in straight and level flight. He put the airplane out of trim and let her trim it repeatedly. After much seesawing on the pitch, she learned to do it well.

"Good. Now we'll practice turns onto headings. I've got the airplane." He glanced at her. She was smiling, obviously pleased with herself. Most of the fear was gone from her eyes.

Showing her how the land below was laid out by fence rows and roads running roughly north, south, east and west, Patten banked the airplane 30 degrees on the attitude indicator and used just enough rudder in the turn to center the ball in the turn and bank instrument to make a coordinated turn while Carley watched. He rolled out on a northerly heading using ground references. He then turned west, and illustrated that a roll-out to a heading had to begin before the heading was reached or the heading would be overshot. He showed her how to use the view of the horizon in the windscreen to keep the bank and attitude constant.

Carley then tried the turns. She would overshoot the assigned headings, climb or descend during the turns, and sometimes use too much or not enough rudder. Her hands were tense on the yoke, and she tended to put sometimes back and sometimes forward pressure, which caused the airplane to climb or descend in the turns.

Patten gently took over again, and demonstrated that light back pressure from two fingers on the yoke was sufficient, when in the turn, to maintain proper attitude.

"You make it look so easy," she said.

"I've had a little more practice than you," he said with a small grin. "You're getting the hang of it!"

She dried her sweaty palms on the legs of her jeans, and practiced assigned turns that Patten called out to her until she became fairly proficient.

"Okay, that's good!" He took the controls. "I've got it. Now, we'll make turns to compass headings using the directional gyroscope. I want you to be looking outside the airplane most of the time, just as you were doing, but take quick glances at the directional gyroscope several times during turns to see where you are in terms of the compass. I'll do it first. We're on a heading of 360 degrees, or north. I'll make a 30 degree bank in a right turn to 180 degrees, or south."

Patten made the turn, and showed Carley on the directional gyroscope where to start the roll-out for a 180-degree heading.

She caught on quickly, and was soon able to make turns within ten degrees of assigned headings and within 100 feet of altitude.

"Very good, Carley. I'll take over now. How are you feeling? If you're not too tired, we'll practice a few climbs and descents to altitude."

"No, I'm fine," she smiled.

"Okay, we're on a heading of 360 degrees. We'll climb from our present altitude of 3,000 feet to 4,000 feet at the best rate of climb speed, which in this airplane is 65 knots. In other words, we'll get to 4,000 feet faster at 65 knots than we would at any other airspeed. Okay, you've got the airplane."

She learned climbs and descents without difficulty. Shortly, she turned to headings he called out for her to follow back to the airport and into the traffic pattern. She gave control back to him on final approach and landing, and she then took over and taxied the airplane back to the FBO.

She parked the airplane, and smiled at Patten. Her arresting eyes met his for a moment, and something…some primordial communication… took place between them that at once they both reacted to but did not fully understand.

Patten was uncomfortable, and averted his eyes while Carley quietly unlatched her seatbelt and shoulder harness and climbed down from the cabin. He began to feel some measure of panic, but fought it by busying himself gathering up the flight paraphernalia and awkwardly exiting the cockpit.

Airplane secured, they silently walked across the ramp to the office. Patten took Carley's student logbook and recorded and signed the flight instruction completed for the day. Turning to Carley, he remarked how she had learned a great deal. More comfortable now, he exchanged smiles with her. Fear was gone from her eyes, and she seemed elated. He then sent her to Linda to schedule her next flight lesson.

"Thanks!" she said. "I can't wait until the next lesson! By the way," she added, "I was at ground school Tuesday night and didn't see you. Do you ever teach ground school?"

"Yes, I do. The flight instructors take turns with ground school. I wasn't scheduled for last Tuesday. I'll have my turn again soon."

"I see," she said. "Well, I'll go schedule my next flight lesson. See you!"

Patten went to his office with mixed emotions. The flight and instruction had involved his mind to the point that his troubles had been temporarily swept to the background. And it was always rewarding to see a new student at first fearful, then gaining rapidly in confidence and competence in handling the aircraft and becoming able to enjoy the pleasure of flight. Now, he was inexplicably saddened by his new student's elation. The warmth of her hip against his in the narrow cockpit also troubled him.

* * *

At Dr. Copeland's office in the early afternoon, Patten described his relationship with his wife and the divorce.

"Janice blamed me for her embarrassment in the community as well as the loss of Steve, and, I guess, rightly so. I was deeply depressed and felt of no value to anyone; consequently I signed the divorce papers her attorney drew up. I took the training to get established in piloting: I wanted to run away from my old profession. I felt a failure and wanted to try to start life anew as a pilot." He was silent for a moment, then added: "It's peculiar, but I feel somehow at home around the airport and airplanes. I didn't feel, and still don't feel, though, able to cope with others except in a work relationship, and even then as little as possible."

"More of an exile than an adventure, I suppose. You wanted to constrict your life—"

"Yes, limit it, to something easier to handle. I didn't want any responsibilities for anyone. I built a wall, I suppose, between all others and me, and I usually felt safe behind that wall. But something's wrong, I seem to be coming unglued!"

"You felt safe behind the wall, but something was missing?"

Patten glanced at the psychologist and felt sudden warmth toward him. "What do you mean?"

"You've functioned well in your work, but you've been unhappy?"

Strong, confusing emotions surged inside Patten's chest. He held his breath and hammered the feelings down. Standing up, he looked at his watch. "I need to go now," he said, in alarm he did not understand.

"We have plenty of time left, if you want to stay longer…Oh…" He raised his eyebrows, "there's nothing wrong with liking me a little, is it?"

"I…need to go," Patten stammered, and left the office without stopping at the receptionist's desk. He drove back to the airport in a daze, very disturbed at the occasional image of a penis entering his mouth; each time the image appeared he gagged and shook his head to clear his mind.

Upon arriving at the FBO, he telephoned Copeland's office and scheduled an appointment for the next day.

* * *

Patten finished the day instructing students and pulling advertising banners along the beach, then left the airport in the early evening. On the way home he picked up a six-pack of beer. At the duplex, he opened a bottle and leaned back in a recliner to relax, but felt restless.

His mind turned to Carley Price. *She is a pleasure to instruct, but she is something special, something that's disturbing.* He drank another beer, felt that he couldn't stand the apartment any longer and went out to sit on the steps, taking a bottle with him.

Melissa Smith, driving up in a red Mercedes convertible, drew him from his reverie. Seeing him, she closed the car door and began putting up the top. It was now only six thirty in the afternoon and she was already 'dressed to kill,' as one woman would say about another. Her red, tight-fitting party dress, high fashion hairdo, jeweled earrings and matching necklace adorned her. She was quite pretty, thought Patten, but somehow he felt sorry for her. Her beauty seemed shallow, a pretty façade covering something not so pretty.

"Hey there, handsome, what are you up to?" she smiled.

"Sitting out watching the grass grow," he tried to be friendly. She had never done anything to him. He didn't dislike her.

"If you have another beer, I'll come and join you," she said.

"I'm afraid I would be poor company," he replied.

"I promise I won't talk much," she countered.

"Maybe later…I was just about to leave," he lied.

"Okay, big boy. Come on over when you get back!" There was a promise of something in her voice.

Sure, with twelve condoms and a wet suit. Then guilt came over him. He felt a strange sort of pity for Melissa, a pity he had felt before. He sensed that her life had no meaning beyond an obsession with male attention. *A succession of men, pretty clothes, flashy sport car—all of the trappings that she hoped would make her happy. And, all to counter the depression lurking underneath. Keep busy with sex, make yourself beautiful, and you don't have time to think about your essential emptiness. That is her way, but, then again, I certainly don't have anything better.*

Patten drove back to Highway 59 South, continued to the end and turned left on Highway 182. He drove past the Lighthouse, and parked at the Gulf State Park Resort. He walked to the beach, carrying what was left of his six-pack.

A low-pressure system was moving in: the wind was strengthening and the air was heavy with moisture. Dark stratus clouds were forming and blowing toward the shore. The winging sea birds, typically very noisy as they crabbed against the wind, were silent on this evening. A solitary ship on the horizon rolled and pitched as it struggled against the current, wind, and waves.

At dusk a lone man walked along the shore, hunkered over against the wind. Patten thought about the conventioneers and tourists who were undoubtedly partying at banquets inside the resort. He saw a couple walking barefoot hand-in-hand at the edge of the water, obviously taking pleasure in each other and the action of the waves rushing over their feet, their happiness overcoming any threat from the weather.

The weight of loneliness suddenly crushed him. He felt insignificant and isolated as he looked beyond the interminable waves and out upon the waters of the Gulf, which stretched as far as the eye could see. He did not recall feeling such loneliness before; anxiety and depression were familiar to him, but not loneliness.

An image abruptly appeared. He was a child of nine or ten years, and as he played in a field an airplane flew over. As it disappeared in the distance a disturbing feeling he didn't then understand—just now he identified it as loneliness or longing—momentarily overwhelmed him. As a child, he had squelched the feeling and had forgotten about it until now.

He sat sipping beer until total darkness came. The white sand usually glistened in the moonlight, but this was a moonless night. The water looked black. He lost himself in the timeless waves cresting and foaming as they rushed ashore.

When Patten eventually glanced at his watch, he saw that it was already half past one. He picked his way through the sparse sea oats to his car and drove back to the duplex. Noting out of the corner of his eye that Melissa had left her living room light on, he entered the duplex, mechanically removed his clothes, and fell in bed.

Chapter Five

Driving back to the airport from Fairhope and his session with Copeland the following morning, Patten felt renewed and hopeful that his problems would be worked out.

Toward the end of the session he had told Dr. Copeland of the loneliness that had flattened him at the beach the day before, and the memory of having the same feeling as a boy on one occasion when he saw an airplane disappearing into the distance. He didn't identify the feeling at the time, but was alarmed and ridded himself of it as quickly as he could. He replayed the interchange in his head, as he did after each session.

"I suppose the plane leaving you caused you to feel, uh…left behind, or deprived?" Copeland suggested.

"Deprived? Of what?"

Dr. Copeland merely looked at him with his kind, blue eyes.

"Well, I don't know…I'd always been interested in airplanes, ever since I could remember. I built model airplanes, with rubber bands hooked on propellers for power, you know, when I was a kid," he said, somewhat embarrassed.

"I wonder if you wanted to go away, to go on that airplane…"

"From…from…from, yes, from unhappiness, unhappiness at home," he sighed.

"You were unhappy, and—"

Patten interrupted, "Yes, and airplanes were a way to get away from the unhappiness, to leave, I guess."

"And…the loneliness?"

"Lonely? Evidently I was, but mother was there, cousins, sister… And yet loneliness overcame me… Of course!" he exclaimed as the realization struck him like a bolt of lightening. "Oh, no!" he said as a wave of emotion overcame him.

Several minutes passed, as Patten was flooded with feelings he had smothered away for years.

Having given the feelings and memories time to run their course, Dr. Copeland said, "I suppose you're saying you felt deprived of a father."

Emotions spent, Patten felt unusually calm, wiped out. "Yes, I did. I couldn't let myself think about it for some reason, I don't know why. But evidently I missed my father much more than I knew. Dad was an airplane pilot in the military. He rarely came home. I was always afraid when he came home. After each slight misbehavior, mother would say, 'Just wait until your father comes home. He'll give you a whipping you won't forget!' I was always afraid of him. I never remember wanting him around, so this is puzzling."

"He passed away a few years ago," he added, after a pause.

"And I'm obviously very lonely now, but I didn't recognize that feeling until yesterday."

"For some reason you covered up those natural feelings for your old man…"

"Yeah, looks like I did."

As he drove through Robertsdale, Patten knew a great deal more work was needed for him to recover memories and to understand how he had become the way he was, but he was optimistic.

* * *

The classroom at Gulf Shores Aviation was typical for a small flight training facility. The walls were decorated with pictures of vintage aircraft, and shirttails of soloed students hung from the cornice around the room. An enlarged aeronautical chart of the United States occupied most of one wall. A blackboard, file cabinets, and folding tables with chairs for 20 students completed the furnishings.

Carley walked in as Patten was in the process of cleaning the blackboard. "Hi, Mr. Fortis," she said merrily as she breezed through the door into the classroom. "You're stuck with ground school tonight, huh?"

He brightened when he saw her. "Oh, hello. Yes, it's my turn. You're a little early. I'm doing some custodial work before we get started."

"I see that. Mind if I just sit in here and wait? Be glad to help if you want."

"Thanks, but I'm almost finished. Have a seat."

"What's the subject for the night?" she asked as she sat down.

"We'll be going over navigation—understanding aeronautical charts, planning cross-country flights, using navigation equipment, and the use of pilotage and dead reckoning to get from one place to another without getting lost—that sort of thing. Let's see, you've had five or six hours of flight training now, so it won't be long until we go on your first cross-country flight, maybe in a week or two if the weather holds. You'll be able to soon use the information we cover tonight."

"That sounds exciting—a cross-country. Where will we go?"

Patten put down the chalkboard erasers and began collating the handouts h'd prepared for the students. "The FAA defines a cross-country flight for a student as one whose destination is at least 50 nautical miles from the home airport. I usually go with students to Montgomery on the first cross-country flight. Montgomery is a controlled airport, which means that it has a control tower, and as a result it gives a student some practice in handling the communications and taxiing procedures in that environment—something more complex than here at Gulf Shores Aviation where we have only one runway and no control tower."

"Flying is more complicated than I thought," Carley said. "When I first started lessons, or even thought about it, I really had my mind on crashing and dying," she laughed. "I still might," she said parenthetically. "But now I think more about everything there is to learn. Do you know what I mean?"

"I think so," Patten said. "Remember, I warned you, there is some drudgery to flying, some book work, and some mental work."

"Yes, you did," she sighed, "and you were right! I was up late last night trying to memorize the one-fifty two manual."

Other students began arriving, and promptly at seven o'clock Patten began the night's lesson. Several times during the lesson, as he was writing on the blackboard while students were practicing the planning of sample cross-country flights, Patten had the feeling of being observed, and when he turned he found Carley's eyes fixed on him. Each time he looked at her, she would smile and look down at her paperwork. On one such occasion, not understanding why she was looking at him, Patten approached her and asked if she understood what she was to do; she replied that she did.

Class broke up at ten o'clock, as scheduled. Patten called out to Carley as she was leaving the classroom and asked her if she would wait a moment.

"Sure," she said as she turned to him, smiling brightly with even white teeth. She approached him and looked at him intently.

He felt uncomfortable with her closeness and attention to him, and backed away. "Uh…Mrs. Price… Carley… I think I failed to tell you that you need to have your flight physical examination in the next few days. You'll need a third class medical certificate on your person when you get ready to solo, which will be a few lessons from now. Linda can give you the name of a local physician approved by the FAA if you call her in the morning."

Her smile faded, "Oh, okay," she said.

"Don't worry about the solo," he said.

"It's not that," she said, rather flatly, as she turned and left the room.

Chapter Six

Chip Summers prepared a personal message banner to tow first, and had it stretched out on the ground when Patten arrived. From fifty feet away, Patten read the five-foot red letters of the banner: "KAREN, WILL YOU MARRY ME? LOVE, JOHN."

He sometimes envied Chip, and sometimes pitied him. Chip was in one relationship after another, and seemed not to want to develop any enduring attachments to any woman. He was 28 years old, blonde, five foot ten inches tall with an athletic build, and seemed to love his bachelor life. He had been on an F-14 maintenance crew in the Air Force on Okinawa for a four-year stint. Because he was found to have insulin-dependent or type one diabetes, he couldn't be licensed to pilot airplanes, but he liked the excitement of being around the, "birds," as he called them, and agreed to work as an airframe/powerplant mechanic and groundman to set up advertising banners for aerial pickup during the peak tourist season. Chip liked the sun, the beaches of the Gulf, lifting weights, and mainly, seducing women, or so he said. The way he talked, Patten wondered if, for him, females were no more than walking semen receptacles. He had been in Gulf Shores only two weeks before joining the Mile High Club, a group whose initiation ceremony consisted of having sex in the back seat of a four-seater while the pilot flew at 5,280 feet above sea level.

Seeing Patten, Chip scratched his head, "Will you look at that, Patten! Another guy, probably completely sane at one time, has now succumbed to the charm of some woman. Why any man would want to give up the bachelor life with the variety of pleasures provided by the beautiful bodies of many females is beyond me—must be a sudden onset of insanity."

"I don't know, Chip. Maybe *you* are the insane one. I've read about sexual addicts…maybe you're one of them," Patten opined.

"Me? No," Chip grinned. "I don't have a sexual addiction; all I want is one woman…at a time. No woman is going to own me! It's not natural. Men were meant to be like stallions, or bulls, over a herd of females," he said, cavalierly. "And, anyway, it wouldn't be right for me to marry and have to withhold myself from all the other good-looking women around."

"Ever thought of moving to Utah?" Patten asked, jokingly.

"Now, that's an idea!"

"Not now, though, I need you here," Patten replied, as he inspected the banner that was stretched out on the grass 500 feet from the runway. All of the connections between the letters were secure. He examined the 250 feet of towline connected to the lead pole of the banner at one end and ended in a great loop at the other end. This, "pickup," loop was stretched between two launch poles, and loosely hung over short plastic rods near the top of the poles. The towline was on the same side of the poles as the banner. All looked in order for Patten to fly low over the launch poles from the opposite side of the banner and snag the pickup loop to lift the banner off the ground.

"Where do I find Karen?" he asked.

"Seahorse Condos. Circle five times between ten and ten thirty, come back, drop that banner, and I'll have another banner ready for you—a restaurant ad. Pull it one hour up and down the coast. After you drop it, I guess we're through for the day," Chip said.

From the hangar storage room Patten took two grapple hooks, each attached to a cable, to the Cherokee one-eighty, and placed one grapple hook/cable on the passenger seat of the one-eighty. He hooked one end of the second cable to a clamp at the bottom of the tail, and stuck one of the arms of the grapple hook into a metal sleeve underneath the cockpit. A small cord was tied around the cable a few feet from the grapple hook end of the cable, and Patten passed the other end of the short cord through a small window on the port side of the airplane, lashing it around the yoke. The cord, held taut, prevented the grapple hook from prematurely dislodging and catching onto anything during the takeoff roll.

When airborne and at a safe altitude, Patten released the cord and allowed the wind pressure on the cable to force the grapple hook from its holder. The grapple hook then stretched out on the cable some twenty-five feet behind and below the airplane.

He leveled off at one hundred feet, dropped one notch of flaps and aimed the nose of the airplane between the launch poles. Throttling back to seventy knots, he descended and was at twenty feet above the ground when the poles disappeared beneath the wings. Pulling the yoke back sharply, he applied full power and climbed out at near stall speed. He felt the pull on the airplane as the grapple hook grabbed the loop, tightened the towline and lifted the banner off the ground. With the extra drag, he had to push the nose down to the horizon to pick up a few knots of airspeed to prevent a stall. He then throttled back in order to keep the airspeed between sixty and seventy knots to prevent a stall on the low side, and damage to the banner on the high side. He circled the airport, slowly climbing to 500 feet, and headed for the Gulf.

"Good launch," Chip said on the radio. "See you in a few minutes."

Patten flew the banner five times around the Seahorse Condos at a quarter past ten. He saw several people around the swimming pool pointing and waving, and felt sure that the message had been delivered to the right person.

Upon returning to the airport launch area, he descended to seventy feet and slowed until the stall warning light flashed red: he wanted to land the banner softly to prevent damage. Pulling the tow release lever, the airplane surged forward as the banner fell almost vertically with the heavy lead pole and grappling hook first striking the earth.

He landed and taxied back to the ramp. Turning the engine off, he crawled out the starboard door, took from the seat the second grapple hook with cable attached and hooked it to the airplane for the second launch.

The second launch went smoothly, and he pulled the banner down the coast from Gulf Shores to Orange Beach and back for the prescribed time. The ground was now heating up and so was the airplane. At the slow airspeed necessary to pull the banner without damage, the engine was barely sufficiently cool, although he kept one notch of wing flaps down to hold the nose level for better airflow around the engine. Thermals were making flying at the necessary airspeed a busy and tiring task, and heat from the engine through the firewall was burning his feet when he returned to the airport.

Chip heard the one-eighty returning and keyed the radio. "Guess what? We have a rush towing job that just came in. Karen is not without humor. Listen to this: SURE, WHEN PEACE COMES TO THE MIDDLE EAST!" Chip laughed. "You're to tow it five times around the

Lighthouse between one and one thirty. I unfastened the other grappling hook and put it on the ramp for you. It's going to take me a few minutes to put the banner together; take a break when you land."

Patten landed and rigged the one-eighty again with the grappling hook and cable. He checked the fuel and saw that he had tanks half full both sides, plenty for another tow.

Linda looked up as he walked into the lobby. "Line one," she said as she gave him one of her practiced smiles, "Mrs. Price." She accentuated the "Mrs."

Patten entered his office and nervously picked up the telephone. "Mrs. Price, this is Patten, what…"

Carley broke in. "Just call me 'Carley'," she said with some uncertainty. "I'm sorry to bother you, but I wonder if you're giving flight lessons today. I may not be able to make our lesson on Monday—babysitter problems—but my son is with his grandmother today. I thought I'd call you just in case you might have some time to fly."

"I've been towing banners today, but I have just one more. Then I have an instrument student." He paused. He didn't want her to develop motion sickness or become afraid again. "You know, the uneven heating of the earth's surface on these hot, summer days creates some turbulence and makes flying at low altitudes in the afternoon a little uncomfortable."

"Is it dangerous?" she asked.

"Oh no…not dangerous at all, but just uncomfortable. The air does smooth out again around six thirty, but that's probably too late for you."

"No, that's fine. I didn't want to wait too long for my next lesson. I might become afraid again," she laughed nervously. "Well, thank you Mr. Fortis. See you at six thirty."

Patten had the flight instructor's typical snack of peanut butter crackers and coffee, then went out on the ramp and fired up the one-eighty. He picked up the last banner without difficulty and pulled it around the Lighthouse hoping John would not be demolished.

Chip was waiting on the ramp when Patten returned. He placed the chocks on the nose wheel when Patten cut the engine. "Not much damage to the banners today," he remarked, "only broke two connecting rods."

"Twelve dollars. Not bad."

As they walked to the office, a Cessna one-fifty pulled up and Rose Martin, a flight instructor, stepped out on the right side. She was an attractive woman of thirty-two, sporting a good figure adorned with auburn hair and large brown eyes. "Hello Patten," she called, "it's getting a little bumpy up there."

"Like a roller coaster, at slow airspeeds," Patten agreed.

"Rose, how are things?" Chip gave her his friendliest smile.

Rose gave Chip a dismissing wave of her hand as she and her student walked off toward the office.

Patten saw Chip's eyes glued on Rose. She was one of the few women that resisted Chip's advances. As Rose walked, though, Patten thought he noticed a slightly exaggerated roll of her hips.

Chip frowned. "That woman won't even give me a 'hello'."

"She's married, Chip," Patten offered.

"That's right, and happily so, as she's told me more than once."

"And, she's probably heard of your reputation."

Patten was puzzled but didn't say anything. When he hired Rose, she told him her husband was an airline pilot and they didn't see each other very often. She said that they each went their own way. Her husband rarely called her at the office, they had no children, and Rose was always working, it seemed. In fact, they were talking about a divorce. And, she was friendly enough with everyone but Chip.

Later, catching Rose alone in the lounge, Patten asked what she thought of Chip.

"He'll be okay when he grows up," she said. "He's not yet out of the habit of thinking with his testicles!"

Chapter Seven

Patten was waiting in the lobby reading an article in *Pilot* magazine when Carley showed up at a quarter after six. He glanced up from the magazine and was stunned. To keep from staring at her, he looked back down at the magazine but had lost his ability to concentrate. Linda looked and rolled her eyes.

Carley was very made up on this occasion, with ruby lipstick and rosy cheeks. Her long black eyelashes accentuated her now pale blue eyes. A red pullover top clung around her full breasts. Her waist was small and hips tight in white slacks.

"Hello," Carley smiled brightly, "thought I'd get here early to do the preflight."

"Sure," Patten finally said, recovering, "you go ahead. I'll be out in a few minutes."

As she walked out the door to the ramp, Patten went to his office to be alone to compose himself. He aimlessly shuffled through the papers on his desk. He gazed out the window and saw Keith, a lineman, pulling the Jet-A truck up to a corporate jet, a Westwind, for refueling. The pilot stood close by, a calculator and manual in his hand.

Patten pondered the aircraft: *This aircraft can take off with a full load of fuel, but can't land until several hundred pounds of fuel are burned off, so the pilot has to be constantly aware of the number of gallons that can be taken on before he violates the landing weight limitation on short hops. He looks in the pilot's operating handbook for rate of fuel consumption at a given power setting, calculates the cruising time, fuel allowance for taxiing, take off, and climb to altitude as well as descent to destination, and with these factors determines the fuel consumption for the trip. He then multiplies the number of gallons to be consumed times the weight per gallon, and then knows how many gallons the aircraft can hold on the ramp before takeoff. Several steps but really a simple matter without the troubling emotions: anger; guilt; love; lust—or all the nuances and combinations of these emotions to consider.*

He saw the lineman stop in his tracks and look across the ramp. Patten changed his position slightly to follow the lineman's line of sight. Carley was balanced with one foot on the foothold of the fuselage, and the other foot on the wing strut while checking the fuel in the starboard wing of the one fifty-two. Chip had exited the hangar door and was also watching Carley.

Damn!

As Patten passed by Linda on his way to the ramp, she smiled sweetly, "I think she's interested in more than flying today!"

He ignored her and walked out onto the ramp where he observed the remainder of the preflight inspection. *Damn, she looks good! Too good!*

"Is it airworthy?" he asked coldly, his unsettling feelings finding immediate vent.

"Everything looks okay," she said, questioningly.

"How many quarts of oil showed on the stick?"

"Five."

"Fuel tanks topped off?"

"Yes."

"What's this greasy, wet spot on the ramp beside the nose wheel?" he demanded.

She shook her head, her mood deflated.

He explained the spot to be only normal condensation from the breather tube, but sharply cautioned her to always look for oil leaks during the preflight.

"I guess I didn't do very well," she said glumly.

Patten now felt angry with himself. He felt guilty at being so hard on her. What in the hell is wrong with me? he wondered.

Strapped in, they taxied out to runway one-eight. Patten had Carley to start using the radio herself. Linda finally answered after the fourth request by Carley for an airport advisory. Patten shrugged his shoulders. Going through the pre-take off checklist, Carley discovered that her door was not fully closed. Sitting against the door, she tried but could not get the leverage to open the door against the prop blast in order to slam the door shut.

"These doors have to be slammed sometimes," Patten said as he reached across her, opened and then forcefully closed the door. As he did so, his arm brushed against her breasts and their eyes locked. Her eyes, for what seemed an eternity, captivated him. There was an aching, a longing feeling that extended from his groin to his chest.

The sensation of movement brought him back to reality: the one fifty-two was taxiing toward the grass on the side of the taxiway. Instructor and student had both released the pressure on the brakes, allowing the airplane to move. Patten pushed on the toe brakes and stopped the airplane.

He face flushed. "I…I'm sorry, I must have taken my toes off the brakes."

"No…I know I was supposed to be holding the brakes." Her look was questioning, and then she smiled as much to herself as to him. "I'll be more careful about that door next time."

Patten was again trying to compose himself and considering calling off the lesson when Carley spoke, "Are we ready to go?"

Surely I can handle this for an hour, he tried to reassure himself. He didn't want to disappoint her, but he felt out of control again. He didn't feel much like an instructor; and felt that he was in some way cheating her, that he was taking her money and couldn't keep his mind on his work.

He put on and hid behind his Aviator sunglasses. "Yes."

They raced down the centerline of one-eight, rotated, and climbed to 1,500 feet. Lingering afternoon thermals gently tossed the airplane about from time to time. Carley had difficulty controlling the altitude until Patten told she didn't have to hold the altitude exactly when flying through the updrafts and downdrafts of the summer evenings.

Patten settled into flight instruction and Carley's enthusiasm with flying helped him recover from his earlier upset. But with the warmth of her hip against his and her heady fragrance, he kept a flight chart spread across his lap.

He had her practice what she had learned: climbs, turns onto headings, straight and level flight, and ground reference maneuvers. He then had her practice landing procedures at altitude.

After what seemed a short time, Patten checked his watch and saw that an hour would be up by the time they arrived back at the airport. Students often became disoriented after making several turns, and needed to be able to find the airport before they soloed, so he asked Carley to see if she could find the airport.

"If you have time," she started, "I would love to fly along the coast, just for fun."

He looked questioningly at her. "…I…I'm sorry, but I have to get back now," he said.

Carley was disappointed, her feelings evident in her face. "Okay, Mr. Fortis, maybe some other time," she said somewhat formally as she turned the Cessna toward the airport. "I don't get out much but today I have a babysitter, and so I'm trying to take full advantage of the freedom," she explained. "Before I started taking flying lessons, I was some kind of a hermit, staying home most always, taking care of Mark, my son, and washing, ironing, cleaning, the whole bit. My social life has consisted of my son, my mother-in-law, cashier at the supermarket, and the pediatrician," she went on, "and that has been most of my life for the past eighteen months."

Patten was silent. He did not want to get personal, and was anxious and wanted to get the one fifty-two on the ground, to leave this woman who was having such an impact on him, to go off alone and seek the security he often found in solitude. He was aware that Carley excited him as no other woman had done since his divorce…actually, maybe forever. Yet he saw nothing but trouble ahead.

He helped her to land the airplane on final and touchdown, with more or less unobtrusive pressure on the flight controls, as the last rays of the sun were barely visible over the western horizon. She had done a good job of finding the airport and negotiating downwind and base legs of the landing pattern. He told her so, and she smiled politely but was quiet. He hurried through securing the airplane in the twilight.

The offices were now deserted. Patten used his key to open the door and let Carley enter in front of him. A dim light from a small lamp cast shadows about the lobby. Patten was acutely aware of Carley in the half-darkness. As she turned toward him, he felt a longing for her that was so strong it threatened to overwhelm him. He looked away. She looked at him, puzzled, and he quickly turned and walked behind the counter.

"I enjoyed the lesson. Do you have time for coffee?" she was almost pleading.

"No...no, I have to be going," he lied awkwardly. He put Carley's time on an invoice and left it on the counter. "Linda can take care of this next week." He rushed over to open the door for her. She paused in the doorway, softly illuminated in the moonlight, and peered back at him in the darkened interior. Her eyes were sad. "I think you don't like me," she commented as she turned and walked out the door.

"No, no...it's not that," he mumbled uneasily after her as he hurriedly locked the door behind them and went to his car.

"See you next week," she called as she slid into her sedan.

He waited until she pulled out of the parking lot before he entered his car. He was still rattled as he turned toward the Gulf, picking up a case of beer on the way to the duplex. Once there, the beer went into the refrigerator; he felt too keyed up to try to relax with a beer. Patten put on his jogging outfit and drove to the state resort. On the beach, he ran barefoot at the edge of the water. Running in the sand was straining, and Patten was panting heavily after thirty minutes.

He fell facedown then rolled over on his back, and lay there spread-eagle staring at the stars until his breathing returned to normal. He tried to think and to make sense about his reaction to Carley. *I must be going utterly crazy. I have enough problems without acting stupid around a new student.*

Pondering a long while, he summed up, to the mental image of sitting across from Copeland, what he thought was his situation: *I'm not married, don't have a girlfriend, and Carley is an attractive woman. But she* is *married, and she's too young, and she's my student. I can't fall all over myself every time I give her a lesson.*

Since his divorce, Patten avoided female relationships. He felt he had enough challenge in dealing with his own emotions. He had forced himself to avoid looking at legs, hips, and breasts, until looking away became automatic. Sure, not long after his divorce, he suffered greatly: the nights were long and lonely when he wasn't working, the prostate pain was hardly bearable—at times he would awaken in severe pain, and jump out of bed to sit in a hot tub of water until the pain subsided. Sex dreams, wet dreams, and the prostate pain diminished over time. He kept a balance of sorts by submerging himself into flying, which at first required his total concentration. It was disconcerting for this hard-won comparative peace and equilibrium to be threatened. He thought that his defenses must be weakening and that he was losing the battle.

He lay, facing upward, on a small mound of sand for some time. On this perfectly clear night, he saw nothing but sky and stars. The Big Dipper seemed close enough to reach up and touch. The vastness of the sky and lack of land reference caused momentary vertigo. He first fought the feeling but then allowed himself to be caught up in a whirlwind of dizziness that he somehow enjoyed, after which he turned his head to bring the horizon into view to end the spinning sensation.

Eventually, brushing the sand off his clothes, he retrieved his shoes, and made his way back to the car. He drove to his apartment, showered, and thumbed through the telephone book. *Carley Price may or may not show up for her lesson on Monday, but she would most likely come to ground school Monday night.* He found Sea Gardens, Incorporated in the telephone directory, dialed the number, and left his number with the answering service.

He had met Ginger Davis when she chartered a flight in a King Air to Miami on a business trip to pick up a load of exotic, and very colorful, tropical fish for Sea Gardens, Inc. The fish were transported in oxygen-filled plastic bags with little water, and fast transportation was necessary in order for the expensive fish to survive. He judged that she was in her mid to late thirties. She had a neat, trim figure, was pleasant, bright, non-demanding and not looking for a husband. She was doing very well as the owner of Sea Gardens Inc. "I don't need a man to take care of me," she had told him in a sincere voice. "I don't want to put a ball and chain on anyone, I just like you," she had said when he hesitated to form more than a business relationship with her. He had shied away from her although she wanted no serious romantic commitment of any kind to anyone. Just the kind of woman Chip looked for, Patten had thought at the time.

The phone soon rang, and Ginger's pleasant and very feminine voice greeted him: "Hi Patten, how's flying?"

"Good," he said, "a little bumpy at low altitude. As I recall, though, you don't fly at all if there is a cumulus cloud within 500 nautical miles."

"That's me!" she laughed. "We'll have another load to pick up in a couple of weeks, Patten. I hope you'll be able to fly me over to Miami again and that the weather will be just as good as it was the last time. That was the smoothest flight I've ever had, and I want you to take me again."

"I'm afraid it had nothing to do with my piloting skills. The air was perfectly smooth; and actually, we were on autopilot most of the time. Just let me know when you want to go."

"You won't convince me," she said. "You handled that airplane as though you were a part of it. Next time, though, I hope we can make a weekend of it. I know some very good restaurants in Miami that I'd like to introduce to you."

"Speaking of eating," he responded to the opening, "I called to see if the offer was still open—you were going to cook me a filet mignon dinner as a perk for getting the fish back alive—although I had little to do with it. Or, maybe you don't remember?"

She perked up. "Yes, I do remember! And the offer is still open. Have you eaten yet tonight?"

"Yes I have," he didn't tell the whole truth. "But is the offer good for tomorrow night?"

"Why, yes it is. Why don't you come over to my place at about…say 7:30 tomorrow evening and I'll polish up my cooking skills. Is filet mignon all right or had you rather have seafood?"

"Filet mignon is fine. It'll be a good change from hamburger."

"How do you like yours cooked? Medium rare is what I like."

"I prefer medium well."

Patten took her address, a beach house on Highway 182 West, and said good-bye until the next day.

Chapter Eight

Patten slept in the next morning until nine o'clock and then treated himself to a breakfast at the Gulf State Park Resort restaurant. He took a seat by the window and enjoyed the view of the expanse of blue water. The restaurant was packed with tourists, who was pointing excitedly at two dolphins swimming up close to shore.

After a leisurely breakfast, Patten drove out to Gulf Shores Aviation for his Sunday schedule of flight instruction. He put in seven hours and was worn out with the heat and afternoon turbulence by five o'clock. He skipped jogging for the day, went to his apartment, showered and tried to doze a few minutes before going to Ginger's beach house. But each time he closed his eyes, he saw Carley.

In the early evening he left his apartment and was not long in finding Ginger's place. He parked between pylons underneath her house. Ginger opened the door as he walked up her front steps. Blonde hair flowed around her thin face. Diamond earrings and necklace ornamented her. She wore a slitted, tight, black evening dress with a top low enough to reveal a well-endowed bust. All in all, she dressed to show off a body she was obviously proud of, but left enough covered to maintain a little mystery. She smiled, revealing sparkling, white and even teeth.

After getting a look at her, Patten suddenly felt shabby in his blue jeans and sport shirt. "You're gorgeous," he said, "but I'm afraid I'm underdressed."

"Don't worry about it; I won't." She replied, delighted. "I'm overdressed, but I don't entertain or get out that often. Your coming here gave me an excuse to wear this outfit I indulged myself in over a year ago."

He looked around admiringly, "You have a beautiful beach house!" Patten was reminded of his previous style of life.

"Glad you like it. Come on in, and I'll show you around." She handed him a glass of wine and took one herself. A bay window looked out upon the Gulf from the first level. On the second level, a door opened to a glassed-in deck overlooking the Gulf, outfitted with a hot tub and large skylights. The beach house was extensively and comfortably decorated.

They enjoyed a pleasant dinner of filet mignon Ginger had prepared so tender it melted in his mouth, a tossed salad, baked potato, and red wine. She had made a sauce of her own design that gave life to the potato. Ginger obviously demanded of herself the diversity of both a successful businesswoman and quality homemaker. She wanted to be a total woman, and to have an appreciation of that fact from others.

After dinner, Patten helped clean off the table and deposit the dishes in the dishwasher. Ginger put on a CD; a piano, violin, and cello combo filled the air with soft, dreamy music. He had played the same music in his car, and found that he could turn the volume up to a point where disturbing thoughts became suspended and his mind flowed with the music.

Afterwards, she took his hand and led him to the couch on the second level. He sat at the end of the couch, and she kicked off her shoes, curled up, and laid her head on his lap. He put his arms around her, pulled her head against his chest, and ran his hand up and down the back of her neck.

"I'm independent, but at times I need cuddling," she said.

"And at times I'm beginning to think I need to cuddle," he replied.

The CD ended, but they still held each other in silence for a long time.

Eventually, Ginger took his hand and led him into the master bedroom. She undressed in the semi-darkness. Patten began undressing, but she stopped him and silently finished undressing him herself. Nude, they crawled into bed and embraced.

Patten looked her over in the soft moonlight filtering through the windows and skylights. She had a perfect figure, silky skin and a full body tan; he found himself wondering if she sunbathed in the nude or used a tanning booth. She was sexually alive, he discovered, as well as intelligent and successful in her work. She told him to relax, and massaged his back. She had no inhibitions; she kissed him all over and ran her fingers around his groin, but he did not respond. It dawned on him that physical beauty in a woman and sexual attractiveness were two different things: he was not attracted to her. He began to feel guilty that she was working so hard, although she seemed to be enjoying herself.

He was on the verge of telling her to give up, that he was out of practice, although she was obviously a sexy woman, when the warmth of Carley's hip pressing against his flashed in his mind. His erection was spontaneous, and he gently rolled Ginger over on her back, and she had an immediate orgasm as he entered her, and again soon after. Yet his movements to him seemed mechanical. He was observing what was going on rather than being a part of it—more an observer than a participant in the act, and he was not able to gain relief. Too, he had a strange sense of guilt as he and Ginger lay side by side afterwards.

"That was so good for me, but I'm afraid not for you," Ginger was the first to speak.

"No fault of yours," Patten said. "I'm afraid I'm not such a good lover."

"I've got no complaints," she replied as she hugged him to her. "And, sometimes good sex takes time."

Ginger obviously had no neurotic concerns such as he, he was sure, as she lay beside him, snuggled up to his shoulder, her arm across his chest and his arm between her breasts. She appeared relaxed and conflict-free. He was envious. Later, at Ginger's suggestion, they entered the hot tub and soaked up the warmth of the water as they enjoyed fresh glasses of wine.

"You've never said much about yourself, Patten," Ginger smiled an engaging smile. "Each time we talk, on the airplane, on the telephone, it has always been small talk, business talk, entertaining talk—now I'd like to know more about you. Some things I see, some things I sense—woman's intuition? I know you're more than you present to people, what little you do present! You're not the average pilot or flight instructor. Who are you?" she asked, interested.

Patten took a sip of wine, and then set the cold glass aside to avoid the heat of the rising steam. "You don't want to know," he said, wanting the conversation to stay shallow. "But I will tell you this, I am a disturbed person, and it would be best for you that you didn't get to know me very well," he smiled, hoping the feeble stab at humor would keep the interchange light.

She laughed. "Well, I know you're not a serial killer! And, sex for you probably involves strong love feelings," she went on. "I know that you don't love me, and that's not necessary for me. I believe that in some ways I'm really not your type of woman. I don't know why you chose me, and why now, since I did let you know I was interested some time ago." She reached over and tenderly ran her fingers across his cheek. "I don't know why, and I'm not asking, but I would like to get to know you better."

"Thanks," he said, feeling uncomfortable with her warmth. He had hoped he could keep this relationship as impersonal as possible. Then, thinking he should say something more, "To tell you the truth, I do appreciate your interest but I'll be more comfortable in keeping things as they are."

"Perhaps later, then. I do hope this won't be our last chance to get to know each other better," she said. "Anyway, if you want to drop it, we will."

He changed the subject. "You have a beautiful view from the hot tub," he said as he sipped the wine and looked out over the waters of the Gulf shimmering in the moonlight.

The clock was pushing two-thirty in the morning when they climbed out of the tub, dried off, and dressed. Ginger walked him to the door. He lightly kissed her lips and started to thank her for the evening when she placed her finger over his lips, pulled his head down and kissed him forcefully again.

"My pleasure. I'll call soon about another trip to Miami."

Chapter Nine

The next morning Patten flew the Cherokee one-eighty along the coast until he spotted Ginger's beach house off the port wing. He throttled back to slow the craft, then dipped the left wing and applied pressure to the right rudder. The cross-control in the early-morning smooth air prevented the airplane from turning, and kept the left wing of the low wing airplane from obstructing his view of the house. Taking his 36-millimeter camera, he quickly aimed the telescopic lens and snapped off a few shots.

He landed and took the roll of film to a nearby photo studio for developing, then returned to the airport and to his office to work on the omnipresent paperwork. However, he was soon called to the lobby by Linda to meet with George Rider, a short, black-headed, moon-faced student in his twenties. George was a heavy equipment operator who came to Foley to help clean up after a hurricane, found that he liked the area and stayed on. George took to flight easily, and his eye, hand, and foot coordination skills acquired operating heavy equipment had transferred readily to airplane piloting. Patten felt comfortable allowing George to solo after only eight hours of instruction. George's difficulty was in the bookwork and navigation required of private pilots.

Patten carefully checked the student's preflight planning for a solo cross-country flight to Tuscaloosa, where George would gain experience in both cross-country flight and operating at an airport with a control tower. Having satisfied himself that George would make the trip successfully, and after giving the student last minute reminders of procedures to use in the event of carburetor icing on these warm, humid days, Patten signed the student off for the flight.

Patten watched George take off down runway one-eight, and was on his way across the ramp to the office when Chip Summers walked up to him.

"Hey, Patten," Chip said as he approached, "I'm afraid I have some bad news. The FAA sent greetings in the form of an airworthiness directive. Came in the mail this morning—an A.D. on the Cherokee one-eighty. The wing spars have to be removed and inspected. It's a major job. We can't do it here but we can get it done in New Orleans. I called the mechanic shop there at Lakeland, which is authorized to perform the service, and the service manager said it would cost $2,150 if no problems were found. The job will take two days."

Although his business was growing, money was tight. Patten was scraping through in the Part 91 Flight School he owned, with some income from banner towing, aerial photography and charter piloting he picked up occasionally. Airworthiness directives from the FAA were always unwelcome surprises, a necessary evil, but this particular one was going to be more expensive than most. "Oh hell, Chip, what's the problem with the spars?" he wanted to know.

"Seems that a one-eighty on an oil pipeline patrol in Alaska lost a wing—fatigue cracks and corrosion were found in the broken spar, which weakened it, and the wing deplaned. Sorry."

"How much time do we have? When is compliance required?"

"The next 25 hours the airplane is flown, or the next scheduled inspection, whichever occurs first, according to the FAA. The one-eighty hasn't flown but 43 hours since its last 100-hour inspection, so it has to be done by 68 hours after the last inspection. I put a sticker near the Hobbs meter to remind us," Chip said.

"Okay, thanks," Patten said as he opened the door to the office. *Nothing like an A.D. to keep your feet, as well as your airplane, on the ground.*

Patten stayed around the office completing paperwork with the vague uneasiness he always felt when students were gone on solo cross-country flights. He felt relieved that afternoon when George called for an airport advisory. Linda finally answered after the third call, "winds 210 degrees at 6 knots, no reported traffic." After debriefing George and rescheduling him, Patten left the airport.

Looking over the negatives of Ginger's beach house at the photo shop on his way home, he picked out one he thought satisfactory and left it to be enlarged and framed. He gave the clerk instructions for it to be mailed to Ginger. On the same roll of film were shots he had taken of property for a realtor, and he had these printed as well and left them to be picked up by the realtor.

Chapter Ten

Flying twice a week and attending ground school two nights a week, Carley had progressed rapidly, Patten thought, as he picked up headphones from his office and walked, with some apprehension, out on the ramp to meet her for her ninth dual instruction lesson. She had no difficulty with ground reference maneuvers or flight with reference only to flight instruments by wearing a hood over her head to blot out all outside visual references. They spent two hours of "touch-and-go," repetitive takeoffs and landings, and she had quickly become skilled at takeoffs and maneuvering in the landing pattern. Although she'd made some landings on her own, she tended to overcontrol on final approach, a minor problem that would be easy to correct. They had completed the required three hours of night flight by going to Mobile and returning, and practicing take offs and landings at night.

She was buckling herself in the Cessna as he approached. Her eyes brightened. "Hello, Mr. Fortis! Ready for another wild ride?"

Her confidence had grown as her piloting skills increased. Because of the decrease in her fear, he felt that she was ready to practice what students dreaded most.

"Good morning. Is this airplane airworthy?" He asked as he walked around and eyeballed the airplane, manipulating the connectors on the elevators and rudder.

"Looks good to me; oil is four quarts on the stick. What do you have planned for me today? More touch-and-goes?"

He entered the cockpit and buckled himself in.

"You're probably getting bored with takeoffs and landings. We'll do something different today…the high work. We'll go to the east practice area, climb to 5,000 feet and practice approach to landing stalls, take-off and departure stalls, flying at minimum controllable airspeed, and steep turns."

Her face turned pale and her eyes widened with fear. "Stalls? I don't know if I'm ready for that."

"Sure you are," he said confidently. "These training airplanes are actually built to bring themselves out of a stall if the pilot just turns loose of everything—but we're going to learn how to recognize an oncoming stall in order to avoid ever having one unintentionally, and learn how to prevent loss of much altitude and heading in recovering from the stall, so we can recover safely if we ever inadvertently stall. You've studied stalls in ground school and in your textbook. You remember the cause of a stall?"

"When you exceed the critical angle of attack between the wing chord and relative wind?"

"Yes. That's good. If the smooth flow of air over the wing breaks up—"

"You fall out of the sky!" she interrupted.

"No," he laughed. "The wings no longer produce lift, and then the nose of the aircraft drops. Then what do you do?"

"You die?"

"Come on!"

"What?" She was too flustered to think, but excited, too, that he thought she was ready for stalls.

"You have to break the stall by decreasing the angle of attack. In an approach-to-landing stall, push the nose down, apply full power, and take one notch of flaps off. As airspeed increases above stall speed, raise the nose to stop the descent, and ease the flaps all the way up while you climb back to your altitude without stalling again. Lastly, return to cruise airspeed and power."

"Easy for you to say," she muttered.

"And you'll find it easy to do, once you do it a few times."

"What if I die the first time?"

"Then you can sue me!" He grinned, and then grimly remembered the one time he *had* been sued, and the smile left his face.

"What?" Carley saw the change in his expression, but was unaware of its meaning.

"Let's get airborne," he said as he put on his headphones.

Carley went through the prestart checklist, called "clear prop!" out her open window, started the engine, and turned on the radios and strobe light. She keyed the mike: "Gulf Shores Unicom, Eight Delta Tango, on the ramp, request airport advisory."

"Gulf Shores Aviation, winds 170 at 5 knots, altimeter setting 29.98, no reported traffic."

"Delta Tango, roger, taxiing to one-eight for departure to the east."

She set the altimeter and taxied to runway one-eight. After completing the take off checklist and scanning the sky for traffic, she announced her intentions, and rolled down the center of the runway.

"When you get to 500 feet, turn to a heading of 110 and climb to 5,000 feet."

"Okay."

Climbing through a hole in a broken layer of stratus clouds at 2,500 feet, they broke through to the bright sunshine bathing the fluffy tops of the clouds that seemed to stretch to infinity. Here and there little cumulus lumps, looking like swirls of cotton candy, protruded up from the undulating stratus carpet.

"Oh, how beautiful!" Carley exclaimed.

"Yes, isn't it?" Patten smiled. "The sun always shines above the clouds!" Surrounded by the stunning fairyland world while flying above the clouds, he often felt guilty about getting paid for work he enjoyed.

"Oh, and look over here!" Carley said excitedly, pointing down and to her left.

He looked where she was pointing, but couldn't see out of her window and down far enough.

"I've got it," he said. He grasped the yoke and dipped the left wing as he applied opposite rudder. Then he saw what riveted her attention. They were flying slightly above and to the right of a cumulus column. A rainbow appeared in the swirl, and the shadow of the airplane floated across the bands of color.

Her eyes met his. "Have you ever seen anything so beautiful!?"

She's enchanted and enchanting. "If I have, I don't remember it," he said as he righted the airplane and returned the controls to Carley. Her eyes made him uncomfortable and he had to look away. Sharing this special moment with her made him again feel a disturbing closeness.

At 5,000 feet, he took the controls and completed a 360-degree turn to look for traffic. Seeing that all was clear, he rolled out on a 360-degree heading.

"I'll do an approach-to-landing stall first, and explain to you what I'm doing as I go along. I first set the airplane up in the landing configuration by pulling the power back to 1700 rpm, turn on the carburetor heat, and as the airplane slows down I maintain altitude by increasing back pressure on the yoke. When the airspeed falls into the white, safe flap operating range on the airspeed indicator, I apply full flaps. As I am slowing down, I continuously increase back pressure to maintain altitude.

"Okay, the stall warning buzzer is sounding, but we're applying more back pressure. The controls are mushy. We're using the rudder pedals to keep the nose on our heading of 360 degrees."

The airplane trembled momentarily. The nose then dropped abruptly.

"Whoops!" Carley shouted.

"Okay. We have the stall," Patten went on calmly. "We ease forward on the yoke as we add in full power, and at the same time take off one notch of flaps. The airspeed is coming back into the white range, and we're no longer losing altitude. We're starting to climb, and so we take another notch of flaps off…we're still climbing, and we take the flaps all the way up. Note that we keep our original heading…level off at 5,000 feet…regain cruise airspeed…and finally throttle back to cruise power."

He glanced at her; she looked pale. "Everything seems complicated at first," he reassured her, "but you'll have no trouble. I'll help you through the first few stalls until you get the hang of it."

"Wow!" she said into the headset. "It's like stepping off a cliff! My stomach is still on the ceiling! My mind was a blank—I don't remember a thing you told me!"

"Don't worry, you'll be okay." He made another clearing turn. "Okay, you've got the airplane. I want you to maintain altitude, but throttle back and use full flaps as though you were flying the final leg of the landing pattern."

She throttled back as she was told, and the airspeed dropped off to the flaps operating range. She carefully slid the flap lever down for full flaps and trimmed the elevator nose down to compensate for the nose up attitude caused by the flaps. As the airspeed decreased, the airplane began descending.

"Hold your altitude," Patten prompted.

She eased the yoke back. The stall-warning buzzer sounded. She was still descending.

"Back on the yoke, back, back, right rudder, keep the wings level…"

The nose dropped suddenly as the airplane lost lift.

"There we go!"

By reflex, Carley jerked back on the yoke to pull the nose up, but the nose dropped more dramatically, and the left wing dipped.

Patten laughed. "Right rudder, yoke forward, full power, one notch of flaps off!"

Carley had her mouth open and was frozen. Patten pushed on the yoke to prompt her as the airspeed was building up close to maximum flap operating range.

She recovered, and loosened up on the yoke while awkwardly pushing in the throttle.

"Good. Now one notch of flaps off and ease the nose up…slowly…another notch of flaps…okay, flaps all the way up."

Patten took over. "I have it. Get your breath while I climb back to 5,000 feet. You'll do fine with practice. We lost about 500 feet before recovery, and we were off course 20 degrees. We'll get better as we go along," he reassured her.

He glanced at her. Her hands were trembling.

"At the stall, remember, nose down, full power, one notch of flaps up. As airspeed builds, flaps full up, and return to altitude and heading."

"Are you sure I can do this?"

"Undoubtedly! As they say, Rome wasn't built in a day!"

"But how long did it take it to burn?"

"We won't crash. I guarantee it!" he laughed.

"If you say so," she replied, not completely convinced.

"You must pick up airspeed to break the stall, and you pick up airspeed by lowering the nose and adding power. Say it after me, nose down, full power, one notch of flaps up!"

"Are you kidding?" she asked.

"No, bear with me. Memorize the procedures first, and you'll learn the action faster, before you go into a stall. Then you'll follow the procedures automatically. Say them!" he urged.

She gave in, "All right: Nose down, full power, and, after that, one notch of flaps up."

"That's correct! After the next stall, say each procedure while you perform it. Okay?"

"You mean out loud?"

"Sure. I want to hear what you're doing. Okay, you have it. We're at 5,000 feet and we'll do another clearing turn before we stall—wouldn't want to run into anyone."

"No, that would ruin our day!" she agreed.

After she learned to handle the approach to landing stalls straight ahead without losing more than 200 feet of altitude and ten degrees of heading, Patten had her to practice the stalls with shallow turns. Then he showed her how to recover from the easier-to-learn takeoff and departure stall, and she was able to recover satisfactorily after three tries.

"That's easy," she said, "but I don't like that high nose-up attitude. You can't see what's in front of you."

"Yes," he agreed, "but it just lasts a few seconds. Now circle and descend back to 5,000 feet—we'll lose the altitude we gained in the take-off and departure stall—and roll out on a heading of 180 degrees. We'll practice flying at minimum controllable airspeed at about five knots above stall speed."

Carley learned quickly how to use power to control altitude and elevator to control airspeed, the mushy feel of the ailerons and the rudder at slow airspeed, how to turn with shallow banks at slow airspeed to avoid stalls and spins, and how to descend and climb at minimum controllable airspeed.

Patten took over. "Okay, I've got the controls. We'll do some steep turns. You'll remember from ground school that, in turns, some of vertical lift on the wings becomes horizontal lift, and the airplane tends to descend, so you must hold more back pressure on the yoke while in turns to remain at altitude. At the same time, drag is increased, and since in the turn the inside wing is moving more slowly through the air than the outside wing, more lift is created on the outside wing and thus the bank tends to increase. You'll counter that tendency by using the ailerons. You'll need 200 rpm more power in the turn to counter the increased drag. I'll show you a steep turn to the right and then to the left. But while turning, look at the horizon in the windscreen for visual reference of 45 degrees bank and stable altitude.

"We're at 5,000 feet, and on a 180 degree heading. We bank 30 degrees with the ailerons, and while we keep the ball in the turn-and-bank indicator centered with the rudder, we pull back on the yoke to increase the bank to 45 degrees. At 45 degrees into the turn, we add 200 rpm more power. Then we grasp the elevator trim at the top and turn it to the bottom, once, then again, and we'll have the right amount of elevator to maintain near altitude at a 45-degree bank. If we start descending, we can make the bank less steep using the ailerons to increase vertical lift, and we climb; if we climb above 5,000 feet, we can increase the bank, decreasing vertical lift and therefore descend.

"Okay. We've almost completed our turn. We gradually roll out on a heading of 180 degrees. As we roll out, horizontal lift is changing to vertical lift, and to keep the airplane from climbing, we push forward on the yoke, decrease power to cruise, and retrim the elevator."

Carley looked bewildered.

"You'll get it. Let's say it first, step-by-step."

When she could repeat the maneuver, he entered a steep turn to the left, and she called out each step before he performed it.

Steep turns with 45-degree banks gave Carley some initial problems. She was uncomfortable in what to her was an extreme tilt of the cockpit, and she tended to descend in the turn. She was unnerved flying into the Cessna's own turbulence in 360-degree and 720-degree turns. After the sixth try, she completed the turns successfully and rolled out without gaining altitude.

"Good going! That was perfect!" He took the controls. "Okay," he added. "I've got it. I'll fly back to the airport—I know you must be tired."

"I won't argue with that. I am tired." She put her hands in her lap and leaned back in the seat. She hadn't realized she had been so tense.

He looked at her, "Maybe I put you through too much today."

"No, I've learned a lot. It was worth it. It's a good tired feeling, if that makes any sense," she smiled contentedly.

"I think I know what you mean," he replied, as his mind turned to Steve's tenth birthday. Patten took him to Amicolola State Park in North Central Georgia. They backpacked 12 miles to the summit of Springer Mountain, the southern terminus of the Appalachian Trail, and arrived soaked with perspiration and drizzling rain. New hiking shoes rubbed heels and toes raw. Steve continued along the trail to fetch water while Patten pitched their two-person tent at the summit among tall hardwood trees and gnarled pines.

The sun came out momentarily through a break in the clouds, and he and Steve took pictures off the top of the cliff looking west from the summit. After they had a meal of beef stew for dinner, they doctored blistered feet, took off wet clothes, and collapsed exhausted on their sleeping bags. A thunderstorm approaching from the West awakened them in the middle of the night. The fierce winds, crashing of uprooted trees, lightning strikes close by, and the large drops of hard-driving rain striking, splintering on, and penetrating the tent made for an all-around miserable and wet night. Steve was scared as they could do nothing but ride out the storm; he finally fell asleep when the thunder diminished.

Patten learned that camping in a tent underneath tall trees on the western summit of a mountain was not the place to be in a thunderstorm. They backpacked three rainy days on the trail, and returned to the park beat, wet, hungry, dirty, and with ponchos hanging in shreds from being torn by the underbrush. Their muscles ached. Their knees were sore from the jarring they took coming down the rocky mountain trail weighed down with backpacks.

Yet, he had felt a sense of accomplishment; he had gotten to know Steve better, and when asked about the trip Patten always replied that he had a good time—miserable but wonderful. He had felt exhausted but contented.

Returning to the airport, Patten logged in Carley's flight time and listed the maneuvers practiced.

"Next time, bring one of your shirts or blouses in, preferably white—one that I can cut," he said, matter-of-factly, as he handed over the logbook. She would soon be ready for the other event most students dreaded.

Her eyes widened. "I'm not going to solo am I? I'm not ready…"

"No," he interrupted. "We've got some more work to do in the pattern, practice emergency procedures, and you'll need to take a short presolo written test. You'll be ready when you solo. Got your medical yet?"

"Well, no," she replied, a concerned look on her face. "But when, when will you want me to solo? I might look relaxed to you up there, but you're with me. I'd probably fall apart by myself!"

"Don't worry. I can't tell you exactly when you'll solo, but I can tell you that you won't solo until you're ready. In the meantime, I've got some artwork to do. The most difficult part of this flight instructor job is doing the drawings on the shirts, you know." He was only half-kidding: he always suffered over the artwork.

"Oh, you!" Her eyes twinkled as she gave him a playful frown.

He smiled. "So bring the shirt in next time. And have Linda give you the pre-solo written test before we fly the next time. Study the one fifty-two manual again prior to taking the test, and you'll have no trouble."

"If you say so, Mr. Fortis. Medical exam, shirt, and solo written test, in that order, right?"

"Right," Patten said, "and have Linda schedule you another flight lesson."

Chapter Eleven

Two weeks later, they had gone over emergency procedures, including loss of power in the landing pattern, and were practicing touch-and-goes. On the fourth approach to landing, Patten noticed that his mind wandered on the final leg, and he lacked the tension in his legs and arms he usually had, being ready to take the controls if necessary.

"Taxi back to the FBO after you land," he said.

She gave him a questioning look but did as he said.

Taxiing up to the FBO, Patten took the controls. "I'll hold the brakes. I need your logbook."

She fished the logbook from her flight bag and handed it to him.

He wrote in the logbook authorization for solo flight and handed it back to her.

"Got your medical certificate with you?"

"Yes, it's in my flight bag," she said, a small tremor in her voice.

"Okay. I'm going to get out here, and I want you to taxi back to the runway and take off and land three times."

She grew pale. "Wait…do you think I'm ready for this?"

"I'm sure you are. You made 100 on your presolo flight test. You've done perfectly well this morning; I couldn't have made better take offs and landings," he said as he took his headphones off, forced the door open against the prop blast, and climbed out. He shoved the door closed and walked with an air of nonchalance across the ramp to the office.

However relaxed he seemed, he was unsettled and watched out the window as Carley taxied the one fifty-two to runway one-eight. But she is ready, he told himself. She will have to go on her own at some point! Patten wondered what was wrong as Carley sat for a long time on the run-up area adjacent to the runway before finally taking off. He worried that the engine was running rough, or there was traffic in the pattern that she might have been waiting for, but eventually realized that she was doing another run-up—he hadn't told her another run-up was unnecessary unless the engine had been shut down.

As she began the take-off roll, Patten ran out on the ramp to a position where he could get a better view of her flight in the pattern. He brought a hand-held radio with him, and listened as Carley reported downwind, base, and final approach. He was relieved as she touched down perfectly for her first landing. He watched her land twice more, and then walked back toward the office to wait for her return to the ramp. But he heard the engine throttle-up, and rushing to the window, saw the one fifty-two taking off again. He stood there as she landed, took off again, and landed again. Finally, he saw her taxiing back to the FBO.

Patten walked up to the one fifty-two as Carley killed the engine and climbed out of the airplane.

"Congratulations!," he said as he walked toward her. They exchanged smiles. "You did it!"

She was laughing as she ran toward him with outstretched arms and yelled, "I did it, I did it, I did it! This calls for a victory hug!"

They hugged each other. Patten was suddenly aware of her closeness, the aroma of her hair and perfume, and, as she squeezed him more tightly, her full breasts pressing against his chest. Feelings began to stir in him, and although he wanted to hold her, he was gripped with anxiety. He suddenly stepped back while pushing lightly against her shoulders. She looked up at him and their eyes met. And some kind of understanding again flashed between them.

"Thanks…thanks for teaching me," she said, flustered herself. "I couldn't have flown by myself without your help!"

As they walked back to the office, Carley knew that she had made Patten uncomfortable, and began to feel pangs of hurt feelings.

"You're an easy person to teach, a natural pilot, really! Anyone could have taught you—mostly you just needed to rid yourself of your fear." He tried to talk calmly, although he felt the urge to get away from her. The problem was, though, that he at the same time was keenly aware of the excitement she stirred in him.

They entered the classroom, and Carley's enthusiasm returned. She was animated and gestured with abandon, "I was scared to death taxiing out to one-eight," she bubbled, "but I went through the checklist on the run-up and locked my mind on what I was supposed to do. Keeping my mind focused on procedure sort of put my fear in the back of my mind, as, I think, you've been trying to teach me. Do you know what I'm saying?" Not waiting for an answer, she continued, "And I took off, adjusted the trim, and it really didn't hit me until I was climbing to the crosswind-turn altitude. I looked out the window, saw the houses and roads becoming smaller, and it struck me: I'm flying! Alone! There is no one else here but me! Mr. Fortis! Help!" she laughed.

Her laughter was contagious. Patten laughed with her.

"And then halfway downwind, I remember, 'Announce downwind on the radio, carburetor heat on, power back to 1700 r.p.m., then, when even with the approach end of the runway, maintain altitude, one notch of flaps when the airspeed slows to the white arc on the airspeed indicator…' I could hear you telling me what to do, as though you were sitting beside me.

"I was so excited when the first landing seemed to be good, at least—"

"It was excellent!" Patten agreed.

"And I took off again, and went through the procedures and I don't think I was afraid anymore after that. I landed and took off and was so hyped up…you know, and suddenly I remembered that you told me to do a certain number of touch-and-goes and I forgot how many…I hadn't counted, and I didn't know how many…"

"Three!"

"…anyway, so I just did a few more and taxied back…What? Three?…Are you kidding me?" She broke up with laughter again.

"Yes…three! I didn't know if you were ever coming down," he laughed. "You'd land, and I'd think, 'Okay, that's it, she'll come taxiing back,' then there you'd go again, speeding down the runway. I began to worry that you'd keep on going until you ran out of fuel."

"You thought I'd be doing touch-and-goes for three-and-a-half hours? Oh, it was just so much fun…I can't tell you how pleased I am, and how much I needed that," she said, more serious now, looking deeply into his eyes.

"You did very well," he said as he took her logbook, opened it and with trembling hand began writing. "Now, I'm writing in your logbook an authorization for you to solo when surface winds are less than ten knots, visibility is five miles or better and the ceiling is 3,000 feet or more. You must take your logbook and your medical certificate with you on each solo flight. Log your flights. The first hour practice touch-and-gos, the second hour perform ground reference maneuvers, and the third hour practice stalls, steep turns and flight at minimum controllable airspeed. After that, we'll take a cross-country flight to Montgomery."

"Montgomery?"

Patten nodded. "Yes, Dannelly Field is the name of the airport there. Do your solo local flights at your own pace, and don't forget to log each flight in your logbook. Call me after you complete those three hours of solo, and we'll plan a cross-country flight." He held up three fingers and grinned. "Three! Okay?"

Carley gathered her flight bag and logbook. "I'll count this time, I promise," she smiled. "I look forward to it!" She strolled to the door, "And thanks again!"

"For what?"

She paused and her now knowing eyes met his, "For helping me conquer my fear. I took flying lessons not so much because I wanted to fly, but I was afraid to fly, and I thought if I could conquer this fear I could face some other things in my life. Do you understand?"

He looked away, "Well, I think so, but you're the one who had the courage to face your fear."

"But I was afraid!," she said, strongly.

"Fear is necessary before courage makes any sense, according to a famous World War I pilot, and I think he was right!"

She mulled that over for a moment. "I guess you're right. But I trusted that you knew what you were doing, and I needed for you to give me a push. So thanks!"

As she moved away, Patten felt a moment of relief that she was going, but also felt a moment of sadness rushing to his chest. An image of a loving couple walking hand in hand along the beach flashed across his mind. Tears welled up in his eyes, and he bit his lip as he entered the lobby to pick up his next student.

At the end of the day, Patten went home with mixed feelings. Hugging Carley felt very good, but anxiety flooded him at the same time.

* * *

Returning from a charter flight a few days later, Patten picked up his telephone messages from Linda. One of the messages was from Carley.

Throwing the other messages aside, his pulse quickened as he dialed her number. He hadn't been able to push the warmth and closeness of her hug out of his mind. He recognized her voice as she answered the ring.

"Hello. Patten Fortis here. You wanted me to call."

"Oh, yes. Been out of town, haven't you?"

"Charter flight. I make one every now and then. How are you doing? Have you taken any of your solo flights?"

"Where did you go?"

He was surprised at her interest, "I flew a couple of businessmen to Owen Roberts International Airport, Grand Cayman Island," he answered. "Just returned."

"That's in the Caribbean, isn't it? How exciting! You live an exciting life. I envy you," she said.

He almost choked. *I've had nothing on my mind but you, and here.*

"I've heard of Grand Cayman..." she continued. "It's a place where rich folks take their money to launder."

He laughed. "That's true, I'm sure. It's a little island in the Caribbean, mostly looks like a resort area: beaches, condos, and the like—large banks and financial institutions, also, though.

"Except for those working for the airlines, pilots as a rule don't have the money to vacation there. When I go I fly in one day, and after that wait around the motel until I'm called and told what time to prepare to fly out the next day. Not very glamorous. I do enjoy the flying and change of scenery. Usually," he added. *But not this time.*

After a momentary pause, Carley asked, with a forced lightness, "Do you get to take your wife with you sometimes?"

Patten hesitated. "I...I don't have a wife. I've been divorced for sometime, uh, Carley."

"Oh, I didn't know!" she said easily.

"Yes, you couldn't have known."

"Well, I guess you're wondering why I called. I wanted to let you know I finished the three hours of solo!" she said cheerfully.

"You did! Already!?"

"Yes, two hours the day before yesterday, and one hour yesterday. It was all right to do two hours in one day, wasn't it?"

"Of course. You're really moving along! How did the flights go? Any problems?"

"They went well, overall. Pancaked on one landing, but everything else went well. I didn't bang up your airplane," she said proudly.

"Mine and the bank's," he said wryly. "Well, that's great! You may turn out to be the next Amelia Earhart, Carley." He liked the sound of her name.

"And you know what happened to her," she laughed.

After a moment, she continued, "Mr. Fortis, I don't want to make a nuisance of myself, but I called to see if we could schedule that first cross-country."

"Sure. I'm glad to see you moving along so well. How about tomorrow?"

"Can we? That would be wonderful!" she said.

"Hold on just a minute."

Patten went to the lobby and took the schedule book from Linda. He saw that two students were scheduled the following morning. However, a charter flight previously planned for the day after had been cancelled.

Returning to his office, he picked up the telephone. "I can go the day after tomorrow if that's okay with you. How about eight-thirty?"

"Fine with me," she said happily. "What do I need to do?"

"Plan the trip as you've practiced in ground school. We'll navigate to Montgomery using pilotage and dead reckoning, with checkpoints about ten nautical miles apart, then we'll use the Montgomey variable omnidirectional receiver—that's a mouthful, so we'll call it the VOR—for navigating the return trip. Have everything ready for filing the flight plan except for the time enroute—we'll have to get the winds aloft report the morning of the flight to allow you to figure the ground speed, time enroute, wind correction angle and heading."

"I'll try," she said, "but it sounds complicated. Would it be okay to call if I have trouble doing the planning? I hate to bother you."

"No bother at all, call if you need to. It sound's complicated, but the more you do it, the simpler it becomes."

"I'll take your word for it, Mr. Fortis."

"See you, then, day after tomorrow."

Chapter Twelve

In Copeland's office, Patten squirmed through an uncomfortably long silence. When he could stand the anxiety no longer, he blurted: "What do you want me to talk about today?"

The psychologist, eyes half closed and leaning back in his overstuffed chair, replied: "I'll just follow along with you—whatever is on your mind."

Patten's anxiety grew through another tortured silence. He looked down at his shoes. Taking a deep breath he started to say something but continued silent.

"Some things are difficult to talk about, huh?"

"Yes." Patten paused for a moment, then said irritably. "As a child, I had to face things alone in school, and in the neighborhood. My mother was always too sick to go to school with me when there were problems, or just when teachers wanted to have a meeting. Of course, my father wasn't there—he was at military bases almost all the time, just running around and having fun, according to my mother."

Copeland's eyebrows rose slightly, and he leaned forward. "Why don't we take a look at your father today, if that suits you?"

Patten's spirits lifted. "Sure. Dad wasn't home very much. I guess my mother had more of an impact on me, growing up.

"I remember her always sick with something or other. She focused on illness a lot—her's as well as others'. Whenever someone came down with something, she thought she had it too. She worried all the time about her health, and worried about us kids. She would become hysterical when we were hurt or sick." Patten then paused for a moment.

"You were remembering something about your mother?"

"Well, yes. I was so frightened that she would become upset when I was sick or had bruises, scrapes, and cuts from the minor accidents all children have, that I didn't go to her when I needed help after I was four or five years old. I would instead try to hide my injuries or go to a neighbor's house for help if I thought my injuries needed adult attention.

"But, you know, I was most bothered when my mother was ill herself," he added.

"Uh huh."

"When I was very young, I was scared that she might die, and leave my sister and me alone. In fact, she often said she might die, and ask—a rhetorical question, I suppose—'what would you do then, because your dad doesn't care about you.' I guess fear is what I felt, fear that we would be completely alone."

Dr. Copeland nodded, "That fear of being abandoned—of not being able to care for yourself, of being helpless and having no parent to take care of your needs—was a real fear in you life."

"Yes." Patten recalled his feelings as a child. "But, it was more than fear, much more. At times this fear was absolute terror!" Patten paused for a moment. "I used to have this dream, over and over again…I dream a lot. Do you think dreams are important?"

Copeland's interest was piqued. "They seem often to be metaphors," he replied, "and help us to understand ourselves."

"I had this dream, beginning when I was a child, and throughout my teenage years. In this dream my mother and I are very frightened because we are being taken by alien creatures into a spaceship aerodrome." He smiled sheepishly, but went on, "The aliens are gigantic, muscular males, with hideous faces—bushy eyebrows, high cheekbones and long fangs. The aliens have captured us and are taking us to the aerodrome. I look at my mother and she suddenly stares at me in horror. I am confused. Then suddenlly I am as a third person, looking at the scene from aloft. I see why mother has withdrawn from me. I am completely terrified to see that I…me…I am one of the alien monsters! I have those sharp, pointed teeth and heavy eyebrows, and my mother recoils from me in terror."

Patten involuntarily shuddered. "I felt completely isolated…, rejected, and in a state of absolute panic!"

After a protracted silence, Copeland said, "In the dream, you saw that you were one of the hated, feared aliens; you were afraid of them and now you're rejected even by your mother, as well as hated and feared by her also—complete abandonment."

"Well, yes, I guess so. I don't know." After a thoughtful pause, Patten said, "In the dream, as it turned out, I was one of them, one of the monsters. I couldn't change it; I was one of those aliens. That was the horrible part, when I realized I was one of them, and my mother saw that I was, and shrank away from me. Yes, that's right! She hated and feared me as she did them!"

The psychologist looked at Patten expectantly.

Patten continued. "I guess she was…I guess…" tears of despair and anger welled up in Patten's eyes as the implication of the dream flooded into consciousness.

The psychologist looked at him with understanding, "Couldn't do anything about that, could you?"

Shortly Patten recovered his composure, but memories swept over him. "My mother and my grandmother, who lived close by and was the matriarch of the family, reminded me often of what a low-life my father was. According to them he was selfish, unfaithful to my mother, and interested more in himself than in us. That point was driven home over and over again. 'Men are no good,' my grandmother would say. Men were blamed for murders, wars, and all the evil in the world. Mother and grandmother were against anything—anything considered manly or masculine, I suppose. I wasn't allowed even to play with toy pistols.

"In contrast, I suppose, mother often confidently and pointedly quoted a passage from the Bible: 'The meek shall inherit the earth.'"

Patten continued associating silently for a moment, then exclaimed, "But, at the same time I was told that I was the 'man of the family' since dad was gone all the time! I heard from one of them, my mother, I think, a story of a woman whose husband was not around, and a son of the family worked and gave his pay to his mother. When the father showed up, the son beat the father. I was a boy, and certainly didn't feel powerful enough to support the family and beat up my father. In fact, I was afraid of him.

"I remember having dreams of my mother being attacked by gangs of men, and I was weak and could not protect her. I vividly remember this one dream. My mother and I are in the house at night. Murderous men surround the house. They have weapons and are going to kill us. Mother is crying for me to protect her. I'm just a child and feel weak and helpless. The men break the door down. I find a pistol and point it at one of the intruders and pull the trigger, but nothing happens. Then I wake up, terrified and feeling guilty."

"A real bind you were in, huh?"

"Yes. I was, uh, supposed to somehow be meek and non-aggressive, and yet even as a child be strong enough to care for and protect the family!"

"And attack and beat up your father, when you were very afraid of him? You felt weak, fearful, and ashamed?"

"Ashamed? Well, yes! I couldn't be what mother wanted me to be..." his voice trailed off.

"Impossible for you," Copeland said in a kind voice.

Patten now felt strong enough to delve into another problem. He took a deep breath. "I, uh, have this student pilot, a woman, that I've instructed for a short time. I guess I, uh, have developed a strong attraction to her...uh, that's giving me trouble," he stammered. "I'm having trouble keeping her off my mind. She's married, but her husband's away most of the time..., months at a time, I think."

The psychologist's eyebrows rose slightly.

Patten continued, "I've kept away from romantic relationships since my divorce, you know. I've not wanted to get involved in relationships, and avoided them, mostly. I didn't want anything like this to happen, especially not with a married woman."

Copeland grinned. "Um hum, and this student brought your gonads alive, huh?"

Patten looked down at his shoes. "Well, yes...I'm having trouble keeping my mind on the instruction, you see. I'm attracted to her and enjoy her company, but at the same time I'm as nervous as a schoolboy around her. And she's paying me to teach her to fly. She came to me to overcome her fear of flying and to learn to fly."

"And how is she doing?"

"Oh, she's a great student! She's a natural pilot. She's lost her fear," he said, and smiled at the thought of Carley.

"Looks like she's getting her money's worth, then. Has she noticed your manliness?"

Patten hesitated, and then smiled. "Well, now that I look back on it, she has been very positive and wants my company. But she really likes flying, and I, well, I thought she was attentive because I am her flight instructor, and she wants to learn more about flying. I don't know. Maybe she has other interests in me."

"But you're feeling guilty, it seems, because you've developed strong sexual feelings toward her that you feel you shouldn't have, or that you don't want to have, if I understand you correctly," he said. "She threatens you, in some way."

"That's right! That's the truth! I'm forty-five years old, and I feel like a teenager around her. She's gorgeous and enthusiastic! She's lively, just the opposite of me. She brings me out of myself. She brings out strong feelings I don't want to have! I get nervous around her and want to run away, and then I feel lonely when she's gone, and can't get her out of my mind."

Dr. Copeland chuckled. "You're *very* attracted to that woman!"

"Right! I don't know what to do."

After a short hesitation, the psychologist arose. "You're making good progress, Patten, but I'm afraid our time is up for today. Perhaps we could take this issue up again next week?"

"I need some help with this problem now! I can't wait until next week!" Patten was adamant and his anger boiled up and overcame him. "Stay with me a few more minutes now. You can do that!"

"I'm sorry."

"You can stay with me a few more minutes. I need to know how to handle this problem!"

Copeland raised his eyebrows, sat back down and leaned toward

Patten. "You're feeling pretty angry at me, now," he said, in a soft voice.

Patten was shaking, and in a cracking voice he shouted, "Yes! I pay good money for these sessions and you owe it to me!" Defiantly he settled back in his chair.

"I'd be interested in hearing more about that."

"Sometimes I think I'm doing all the work here! I talk! Spill my guts to you and all you can say is 'uh huh.' And then when I do ask you for something, you don't have the time!"

"You feel I let you down, and don't hold to my part in this relationship."

"Yes! That's right. And you want me to criticize my mother! But I'll tell you this: she stayed with us and took care of us while dad was doing 'God knows what' around the country! *He* probably ran around with married women!"

Dr. Copeland broke a long pause. "I appreciate your telling me your feelings, Patten. If you have anything else you wish to say about that, I'd like to hear it," he said, gently.

"No, that's about all," Patten replied. His anger diminished as quickly as it had arisen.

"I'm sorry I have no more time now. How about late this evening, or tomorrow? I do understand your need to talk more about this issue soon."

"Could you this evening, maybe seven o'clock or so?"

"Sure. I'll be glad to. See you at seven, then."

Patten's mood was elevated as he drove through Spring Hill and Robertsdale on his way back to the airport. Before reaching the airport, he picked up his cell phone: "Hello, Ruth. This is Patten Fortis. I don't have anything to talk about that can't wait. I won't need to see Dr. Copeland this evening, so cancel the seven o'clock appointment. By the way, I'm glad to see he's not limping now, seems to be getting around better. Has he had the hip fixed?"

"Limping?" She hesitated a moment. "Oh, that problem seems to be intermittent, comes and goes."

"Huh! Well, does he have an opening for next week?"

* * *

After dropping a banner, Patten turned downwind to approach for landing at Gulf Shores Aviation, and reported his position over the Unicom frequency. Moments later, he heard over the radio an aircraft reporting a one mile straight-in final for runway one-eight. Patten scanned the sky to the north but could see no aircraft.

He keyed the mike, "Gulf Shores traffic, Four Lima turning base for one-eight."

A cocky voice blasted through Patten's headphones. "Four Lima, Two X-Ray Tango final for one-eight. Move out of the traffic pattern!"

"Two X-Ray Tango, Four Lima, do not have you in sight. What is your position?" Patten demanded.

"X-Ray Tango final for one-eight! Clear the traffic pattern!"

"X-Ray Tango, Four Lima. Turning northeast to extend downwind leg to avoid possible collision. Will see you on the ground, Bud!" Patten said sharply.

A student in a training airplane then reported entering an extended downwind leg for landing, also.

Patten flew two miles northeast of the airport before eyeing a King Air descending for a landing on one-eight. He brought the Cherokee around for final approach behind the King Air after announcing on the radio that Four Lima would be second to land.

As Patten taxied the Cherokee up to the FBO, the last of the passengers was stepping out of the King Air and making their way across the ramp to the FBO.

Patten parked the Cherokee and approached a man who was placing a cover on the King's pitot tube. The man had short-cropped blond hair and a thin mustache. He wore a light blue shirt with shoulder epaulets and dark blue trousers.

"You the pilot of this airplane?" Patten asked.

"Yeah. Who are you?"

"Patten Fortis, pilot of Four Lima. I don't like one bit the way you came into the airport Bud…"

"Wait a minute," the pilot interrupted. "The name's Chuck Ward. This is an uncontrolled airport, and I reported final approach!"

"Reported final approach? From where? The moon?" Patten said hotly. "You must have been a good twenty miles or more out when you first reported! You tied up everyone else so that you wouldn't have to take the time to fly the normal traffic pattern! What makes you think you're entitled to make everyone else wait for you? Just who do you think you are, Bud?"

"I didn't violate any FAA rules—and I told you my name," the King Air pilot said defiantly, but took a step backwards.

"You know as well as I do that straight-in approaches are not recommended because they're more likely to result in collisions. And Four Lima was at a lower altitude, is slower than this King Air, and was closer to the runway. My copy of the FAA regulations states that the lower, slower, or closer aircraft have the right of way, Bud. What about yours, or haven't you read the regs lately? Maybe you'd like for me to make a complaint to the FSDO, and have them read you the rules? How would that look on your record?"

"Now…maybe you're right," the pilot said, more compliantly. "I wouldn't want any complaint on my record." He sighed. "You see, it's like this: the boss is in a hurry to get on the ground and make his business meetings. He doesn't want to wait on anyone. He's always a few minutes late in getting started, and then pressures me to make up the time."

Patten cooled down a little. "Maybe you need to explain to your boss about safety and good manners in aviation. Others may be in a hurry to land, too, and their reasons are as important as those of your boss!"

"I can talk to him," the pilot said contritely. "Will that fix the problem?" he asked.

"You're the pilot. You're ultimately responsible for how the airplane is flown. Do what you have to do, but take care of the problem!"

"Yeah, okay." The pilot looked relieved. "I'll fly the traffic pattern next time."

Patten still felt hot but he returned to the one-eighty and tied it down.

Upon entering the lobby, through narrowed eyes Patten saw a man leaning over the counter angrily shaking an index finger at Leland Robertson, owner of the FBO. A woman stood behind him with luggage at her feet. The lobby was full of students, instructors, and customers whose attention was riveted to the person at the counter. Linda was watching intently, enjoying the show.

The loud man, who was dressed in brightly colored shorts and shirt, was saying, "…know my rights! This airport gets federal funds, and is therefore open to the public. You can't charge me to land here. I won't pay it! It's a rip off!" He glanced over his shoulder and exchanged a look with a woman behind him, obviously pleased with himself and his show of boldness. "Shirley, these Alabama hicks are trying to rip us off at this two-bit airport!"

Leland spoke patiently, trying to calm the man. "I told you, Mr.

Horton, this is a private airport. We don't receive any federal operating funds. The landing fee is published and is only $15.00. We've taken on the liability of looking after your Lance for a week. The landing fee is little to ask in return, and the fee is waived if you purchase fuel." However, the guy would not be calmed because he was enjoying the limelight too much.

Before Patten realized what he was doing, he had crossed the lobby, grabbed Horton by the shoulders, spun him around, and put his right forearm under the guy's chin, jamming his head down to the counter.

Patten put his mouth an inch away from the surprised man's ear: "Listen asshole, the only thing this airport and the 'Alabama hicks' lack here is snobs! You're here now, so we have everything. It's simple: pay the landing fee or top it off!" he hissed through clenched teeth. "Which will it be?"

"Okay, okay, mister...I'll buy fuel..." he choked.

Patten relaxed his forearm. Horton straightened up, coughing.

"Leland, where can he find the lineman?" Patten asked.

Leland, surprised, stood up behind the counter. "He's out on the ramp, Patten."

Patten turned back to the now red-faced man. "Find the lineman and tell him what you want!" he ordered.

"Okay, all right," he said deferentially as he picked up the luggage and headed for the ramp. "Come on, Shirley! We'll never come back here again!" he shouted toward the lobby, having recovered some of his courage with growing distance from Patten.

Shirley had stepped back, her hand over her open mouth. She nervously collected her purse and followed through the door to the ramp.

Linda, eyes wide, watched Patten as he returned to his office. The lobby occupants smiled at each other.

Patten, shaking with anger, sat down at his desk and held his head in his hands, waiting for the adrenaline to subside. *What in the hell has come over me?* he asked himself.

In a few minutes, he buzzed Linda on the intercom, "Linda, ask Leland to come to my office if he has a few minutes."

"Yes sir."

After a few moments, Leland knocked and opened Patten's office door.

"Leland," Patten said, "I want to apologize for losing it out there. I don't know what came over me…"

"Patten, you don't owe anyone any apologies. You did what I would like to have done," Leland grinned. "You know, I get tired of 'the customer is always right' kind of bullshit. The guy was putting on a show at my expense, and you ended it. Thanks."

"You may have lost a customer. You're not ready to run me off?"

"Not at all! Really, I would sell-out if I had to put up with customers like him all the time. His type always wants something for nothing. I can do without them. I didn't expect it from you, though, so it kind of shocked me. You're always levelheaded, so professional—I was just surprised, that's all. Not half as surprised as Horton, though," he laughed.

Patten, relaxed now, looked evenly at Leland, "Well, thanks."

"No, thank *you*, Patten," Leland said as he took Patten's hand and shook it.

Chapter Thirteen

The next day Patten found himself brooding in his office. He had been struggling most of the night to keep his mind off Carley Price. He tried to concentrate on the paperwork on his desk, but would find himself reliving the scent of her hair, the sound of her laughter, or the excitement of having her pressed against him.

The sudden buzzing of the intercom startled him. "You have a telephone call," Linda said in a sing-song voice.

Patten picked up the telephone, and perked up when he recognized the voice on the other end of the line.

"Mr. Fortis," Carley said, "I'm having trouble planning the cross-country trip, the navigation part. I hope I'm not bothering you. You're going to think I'm stupid!"

"No, not at all," he said. "Planning a cross-country is difficult. I'm glad you called. What is it that's giving you trouble?"

"Heading, course, magnetic, true. I get them all mixed up. You asked me to plan a trip to Montgomery from Gulf Shores. I remember that I first line up the plotter on the aeronautical chart from our airport to the Montgomery Airport. I know how to use the plotter to figure something, but I don't know what it's called. Do you know what I mean? Do you understand."

Patten could talk to her more comfortably on the telephone than in person: he felt more in control at a distance. "Okay. I believe I understand. You use the plotter first to measure the distance between the two airports, in aeronautical miles. You then use the plotter to determine true course, that is, your course to the destination airport, Montgomery, in relation to the geographic North Pole. To change that to magnetic course, so you'll know the course with respect to magnetic North—the way the compass points—you'll add or subtract the magnetic variation. Remember 'East is least and West is best,' that is, subtract eastward variation and add westward variation to the true course in order to come up with the magnetic course. You get the variation from those small dashed lines, isogonic lines, which run diagonally across the chart. True course plus or minus variation is the magnetic course. Then, to get the magnetic heading, or the heading toward which you'll fly the airplane, you have to…"

"Mr. Fortis?"

"take wind correction and any compass deviation into account. Magnetic course, plus or minus the wind correction angle, plus or minus compass deviation, gives you the magnetic heading. The magnetic heading is the heading you should fly on your directional gyroscope to reach Danelly Field in Montgomery if you're flying direct from Gulf Shores Aviation."

"Mr. Fortis?"

He finally realized that she was trying to get his attention. "Yes?"

After a moment of silence, she sighed, "Thanks. I just didn't understand that dumb variation."

There was another pause, and he felt her near. They held the telephone connection for a long while, neither saying anything. He felt her presence and was lost in his feelings when she spoke, in a measured voice, softly and slowly and with a touch of sadness, "I'm leaving next Saturday to visit my aunt in Atlanta, with Mark…I wish you were going with us…, but I guess that's impossible, isn't it?" A short electrified silence ensued.

With the sound of those words ringing in his head, he was momentarily speechless, but then Patten's bottled up feelings broke through, as would a tsunami over a footprint in the sand. "Oh Carley. I don't know anything I'd rather do," he blurted out. "I haven't been able to get you out of my mind. I don't know what to do. I'm sorry. I can't keep my distance from you. You've become too important to me. My mood rises and falls based upon whether I see you or talk to you. I can't continue to give you flight instruction. I've just tried to fight my feelings and lost. I've done all I know to do," he said, resignedly. "You're paying for flight instruction; you deserve someone who can keep his mind on his work."

Carley was silent for a moment. "Oh no, don't be sorry. I…I'm not displeased, just puzzled. I wasn't sure you even liked me." She was silent for a moment. "I've really wanted to hear this for so long! And now, I don't know what to say."

"I'm sorry," he repeated. "I know you're married, of course, and you have a son. I…I've struggled with this thing for a long time, and I can't keep my mind on my work with you. Something's wrong with me. I just can't do it. The only thing I know to do is to transfer you to one of the other flight instructors. They're all very good. You've met them all in ground school. You choose one, and I'll make a transfer," he sighed, as he was filled with chagrin to think that he wouldn't see her again.

"I'm married on paper only…I had no idea you felt that way the…No, I don't want another flight instructor…" She then suddenly lashed out, her voice choked with emotion. "I hope you're not just trying to get rid of me!"

"Please don't misunderstand. Don't you see? The last thing I want to do is to get rid of you," he whispered hoarsely into the phone, desperate to make her understand, to relieve her of her hurt feelings.

Hearing the anguish in his voice, and now angry with herself, she said, "Oh, I'm so stupid! I just wasn't sure why you wanted to transfer me." Then, after a short pause, she asked: "Do you have time for me to come by and see you a few minutes today...this afternoon? I think we need to talk."

"Sure," his heart raced at the thought of seeing her. "Is two o'clock okay?"

She recovered more quickly than he. "GMT or CST?" she asked jocularly.

In spite of his turmoil, he laughed, "You did learn the time zones well! Let's keep this thing 'local.'"

As he later thought about it, he had mixed feelings about seeing Carley. He wanted to see her but his head told him that he should not, as she was married. It wasn't unusual for a student to become infatuated with a flight instructor, though such students were usually younger than Carley. He had generally just shrugged off such advances, kept focused on flight instruction, and the student was then able to keep her feelings in line. This time was different, because *he* had strong feelings and his control had failed him. Further, he realized he wasn't sure he wanted to control his feelings any more. At the same time, he felt absolutely elated, at the peak of happiness, that she wanted him to go with her and her son to Atlanta. But then again, she also thought it impossible for some reason or other. And the possibility or impossibility led him into a feeling of puzzled dispair.

All of these feelings churned together. As the time for Carley to arrive drew near, Patten was more of a mass of anxiety than anything else. The time had snailed along, agonizingly slowly. He had been unable to concentrate on the computer or any of the paperwork that hid his desk, and as the time approached, he found himself looking through the window toward the parking lot to watch for Carley's automobile.

In time he saw her arrive, and he rushed to the lobby to greet her at the door so that she wouldn't have to explain her presence to Linda.

Carley breezed in with an air of excitement about her, excitement mixed with puzzlement. Her movements were impulsive but coordinated. She radiated beauty and excitement, outfitted in a red dress, matching scarf, earrings, and touch of pink on her cheeks. Her hair was immaculate. Linda looked at Carley on this occasion with envy instead of the disdain she had felt at their first meeting.

"Hi," Patten smiled, his heavy thoughts having been completely obliterated by the shock of Carley's presence. "Let's go back to my office."

Patten fumbled with the doorknob and felt awkward and obvious in trying to avoid any physical contact with Carley as she walked through the doorway past him into his office.

Once he closed the door, he was surprised that she had not sat down but stood looking at him. He was amazed at her control and apparent confidence, compared to his own feelings of utter incompetence. As he turned from the door, she reached out and tenderly took both of his hands in hers. Her hands were hot, and electric impulses shot up his arms from her hands; his scalp tingled. She drew him close and hugged him. He made a weak effort to pull back from her. She clasped him tightly against her body, and moved her head back from his chest to meet his eyes. Her eyes were misty with feeling. She closed her eyes, and moved her lips toward his. Instead of kissing her, he avoided her lips, pushed his head down beside hers to her shoulder and moved his body back so that she would not feel him rising against her.

Carley gently lifted his head. Her eyes, now filled with tears, met his. "Kiss me," she pleaded.

His conflict still exerted some weak control as he kissed her lightly on the lips. He felt her press harder against him, her tongue warm and soft searching for the inside of his lips, and his resolve was no more. His mind reeled. He momentarily felt dizzy and staggered, but caught his balance. He then responded passionately, his heart racing, his breathing quick.

She held tightly onto him, her body became slack, and she leaned against him. She wept softly as he held her head against his chest. "You don't know how much I've wanted this," she said.

He was stunned at the intensity of her feelings. "Oh God! You too? If you feel this way, too, there's no hope! I never thought you'd be feeling the same way. And you're married! I gave up on love a long time ago—I'm no good at it. Not good with people at all!"

"I...now I just come here to see you anyway," she confessed. "The fear of flying is gone. I just come here to see you!"

"To tell you the truth, I feel the same way. I don't want you to be away from me."

"I wish you could go to Atlanta with me. We need some time together to talk, away from here. Is there any way?"

"I don't know. When are you returning?" he asked.

"Sunday afternoon. I plan to stay just one night."

"Well, hold on a minute," he said as he reached for the doorknob.

But Carley gently pulled his hand away. She took a tissue out of her purse and wiped his lips. "Now you look more presentable," she smiled.

Patten closed the door behind him and shortly returned with his schedule book. He found Carley touching up her lipstick.

"I can move some things over to late Sunday," he said. "But I won't be able to leave until six p.m. Saturday." He thought for a moment. "If we take the Aztec we'll arrive there before you would if you left driving at noon."

"What kind of airplane is the Aztec?"

"It's a twin. Seats five. We probably couldn't get clearance into Hartselle International, but we could fly to Charlie Brown Airport."

"Where?"

"Charlie Brown," he laughed. "People don't believe you when you tell them the name of the airport…but no kidding, that's the name. It's northwest of the city. We can take a motel shuttle to my motel, and then you and Mark can get a taxi to your aunt's."

"Good. Then I'll see you tomorrow for the cross-country," Carley said as she smiled and opened the door.

But Patten closed the door. "Carley, wait a minute. Look, we've got the flight training," he sighed, "mundane as it is compared to holding you. If you want me to continue to instruct you, and to do an adequate job, I'm going to need your help to stay focused on flight instruction while I'm with you. Will you help me put our other relationhship, whatever it may turn out to be, on hold while we're working on your private pilot license? As you see, my will power is obviously totally insufficient around you."

She smiled brightly. "And I'm so pleased you feel that way. I'll have difficulty, too. I promise to try and keep my distance, although I *will* have a problem trying to keep my hands off you."

Patten accompanied Carley as she walked across the lobby to the door. As she opened the door, she turned, smiled at him, and pulled the door shut behind her.

Patten saw Linda staring at him suspiciously. He became self-conscious and quickly went back to his office and closed the door.

But not even Linda could spoil this moment for him. He treasured the taste of Carley's lipstick on his tongue, and the aroma of her perfume on his hands. He was filled with elation mixed with foreboding. He didn't remember feeling this happy in his entire life. He felt himself lucky, though he did not understand why Carley, a beautiful, grown, married woman with a young child, would be interested in him.

He called Linda on the intercom: "Linda, put me on the schedule for the Aztec from six p.m. Saturday until four p.m. next Sunday. And move my students for next Saturday over to Sunday, after four p.m."

"Okay. Where are you going in the twin?"

"Flying!" He hung up quickly.

Chapter Fourteen

The excitement of holding Carley was too much to allow for any sleep, but Patten nonetheless felt energized and enthusiastic the following morning. Both he and Carley arrived early at the airport for the planned cross-country flight, and both had difficulty keeping the instructor-student role in focus. He wanted to hold her, but kept his distance. She seemed hurt initially, but recalled the agreement, and smiled when he said: "Remember…the flying!"

The flight service station reported a 10-knot wind from 315 degrees at 3,000 feet. Carley used the wind direction and speed to complete her calculations and, with Patten's help, filed a flight plan to Montgomery. After reviewing her flight planning, they departed Gulf Shores Aviation. Climbing to 3,500 feet while crabbing into the wind, Carley began looking for checkpoints—highways, power lines, towers, or railroad tracks—to keep up with her position. She had previously marked and measured distances between checkpoints on the aeronautical chart, and used her flight computer to calculate actual ground speed by clocking the flight time between two checkpoints, a crossroads and a tower, and comparing the flight time to the distance between the checkpoints. Patten checked her computations and found them flawless.

"Very good! We won't need the flight computer again," he said, thus relieving her of some of the paraphernalia in her lap and hands. "You have the ground speed check down pat. Navigation will be easier on the return trip since we'll follow the MGM VOR until the signal is too weak for navigation, then we'll get a radar vector to Gulf Shores Aviation."

Carley stuffed the flight computer into her flight bag. "Thanks. You need four hands to fly with all the cross-country chores to do."

Relaxing a moment from the tension of flight preparation and the workload of flying and navigation on the cross-country trip enough to notice her surroundings, she exclaimed "It's a gorgeous morning!" as her eyes swept the bright expanse of blue sky, dotted here and there by small, puffy cumuli. Mares' tails swept out high above, reminding her of angel hair.

Patten was caught up in her enjoyment of the moment and felt warm toward her. He glanced at her eyes behind her sunglasses as she looked out the port window. Her eyes were now pale blue.

Twenty miles southwest of Montgomery, they listened in on the ATIS—automated terminal information service—frequency for surface winds, altimeter setting, and runway to expect for landing, and, as instructed, called Montgomery approach to announce their position and intentions. Approach designated a code to set on the transponder so that the aircraft would be easily identified on the controller's radar screen. When the airport was in sight, approach control switched them over to Montgomery tower to receive landing instructions. As they were descending, Patten pointed out the VOR transmitter on the ground; it was shaped like an inverted wedding cake. Once on the runway, tower switched them to ground frequency, and ground control directed them to an FBO.

Carley kept up with the change in radio frequencies without difficulty, as she had already listed the frequencies on the back of her flight plan. She needed a little help from Patten in finding her way on the ground. Patten complimented her on her performance.

Having given the lineman instructions to top off the Cessna, Carley and Patten entered the clean and attractively decorated FBO.

"We'd better call the flight service station and close out the flight plan—they do get upset and may yell at you if you forget to close out the plan, because they have to start search procedures!" Patten said as he vividly remembered one such incident involving a student a few months back.

Carley telephoned the flight service station and closed out the flight plan. She and Patten took a short break for some popcorn, a cup of coffee, and a visit to the restroom. They then made a short visit to Montgomery tower to familiarize Carley with the work of flight controllers. Shortly afterward, Carley filed a return flight plan, Having paid for the fuel, they strapped themselves in the one fifty-two for the return trip.

They listened to the updated terminal information on the ATIS frequency, and then switched to the delivery control frequency, where they were given a new code for the transponder as well as runway instructions. Carley started the engine and advised ground control that they were ready to taxi. Ground gave them clearance to taxi to the runway, after which tower gave them permission to take off. Once airborne, they were switched to the departure frequency. They made their way to the 215 radial of the MGM VOR and followed the needle on the VOR receiver toward Gulf Shores Aviation. When they were out of the usable range of the MGM VOR, Patten had Carley obtain radar following for collision avoidance and eventual vectoring to Gulf Shores Aviation. Carley also practiced calling flight watch for updated weather reports while enroute, and flew for 20 minutes under the hood, which limited vision to the cockpit instruments, in order to simulate flying in clouds.

Back at Gulf Shores Aviation, alone in the flight instruction room, Carley closed out her flight plan and Patten entered the flight into her logbook.

"Well, that was fun!" Carley exclaimed. "What do I do next?"

Patten was surprised at her lack of fatigue. "Aren't you tired?"

"Maybe a little," she admitted. "But it's another good tired feeling. I *am* a bit tired, but I feel great! Does that make any sense? Do you know what I mean?"

"I think I do…of course I do."

He quickly pulled her close. "I'm sorry. I can't help myself," he apologized as he kissed her cheek then backed away.

Her eyes grew moist. "You're forgiven. Do it again!" she said.

He held her again for a moment, and she hugged him tightly.

"This is difficult. What are we going to do?" asked Patten.

"Go to Atlanta?" she laughed, but with a serious undertone.

"That's a few days away. Seems like forever."

"Could we fly again tomorrow?"

He stepped back away from her. "You don't need much more in the way of dual instruction," he said, with a touch of sadness. "Would you like to take one of your solo cross-country flights tomorrow, weather permitting? You really should take your required three solo cross-country flights before we fly together again."

"Okay. I'll take one tomorrow, then. I want to get this out of the way. I'm in a hurry to focus on our 'other' relationship."

"Why don't you plan a cross-country to Monroeville for tomorrow? There is a VOR transmitter right at the airport. Navigate by VOR there and back, but keep up with your position on the aeronautical chart, and make one ground speed check."

"You think I'll get lost, don't you?" she feigned a small hurt.

He ignored her question. "And, I want you to get radar following there and back—sometimes there's helicopter traffic in the Pensacola North MOA, the military operations area you'll be flying through—and I want you to telephone me when you get there. If you can't get me, leave a message with Linda!"

He touched her hand. "I worry some about all my students, Carley, but you've become very special to me," he said softly.

Her eyes, deep blue now, grew moist and serious. "I think I'm going to cry."

Linda interrupted on the intercom. Patten's next student had preflighted the one fifty-two and was ready to go.

Carley wiped her eyes. "I'll go then! See you tomorrow. Twelve o'clock, okay?"

"That's good for me, but you'll have to cope with light turbulence. See you then."

* * *

Patten met Carley at noon the next day. Finding her flight planning correct after the weather was checked, he wrote the authorization for the solo flight in her logbook. He watched her depart one-eight and he then entered his office planning to work on the Internet and to attack a large pile of paperwork on his desk. Unable to concentrate, however, he nervously paced the floor until his next student arrived. Before he went to the ramp he left word for Linda to radio him as soon as she heard from Carley.

Patten was returning to the airport with a student when Linda called and informed him in a sarcastic voice that Mrs. Price had telephoned from Monroeville, was having no problems, and that she would be taking off again shortly for the return trip. He enjoyed a few moments of relief, but the worry built up again when he thought of her return flight.

It was after four o'clock in the afternoon when Patten heard Carley on the radio returning to Gulf Shores Aviation. By the time he finished the flight lesson and landed, Carley had left the airport. He went to his office and called her home but got no answer. He telephoned her later and found her cheerful and pleased, although she wished, she said, he had been with her. She wanted to know if she could take another cross-country flight on Thursday.

"Carley, I don't know if my nerves can handle that so soon!"

"I'm happy you care about me Patten, but don't worry. I'm a big girl. You've taught me well. Now help me to finish these cross-countries so I can get back with you."

Patten agreed that there was no reason to delay and hurried out to the desk and reserved the one fifty-two for her.

Returning to his office, he picked up the telephone again. "Now don't tell me you're going to want to go on the final solo cross-country on Friday, Carley."

She laughed. "There you go reading my mind… And why not?"

"I told you not to tell me!"

"Come on! Is the one fifty-two available?"

"A couple of students are scheduled, but I can probably move them to different times, one earlier and one later. You realize that this will be your long cross-country, 250 nautical miles, and landing at two other airports—it will take almost all day."

"No problem for me. Mark is in daycare in the morning and a sitter can be arranged on Friday afternoon."

Patten sighed.

"What's wrong, is something wrong?"

He paused. "Nothing."

"Yes there is! What's wrong?"

"I feel a bit silly."

"Why?"

"I just felt sad. It occurred to me that you're finishing up your flight instruction so quickly…you're finishing up and I might not see you again."

"Do you mind if I call you a dummy?"

"I've been called worse," he said glumly.

"Listen, dummy, why do you think I want to finish the solo cross-countries so quickly? Huh? To be with you, that's why…for dual instruction again. That's all I think about. You! And if I have to fly solo day and night to get to that point, I will!"

"Really?" He felt his face flush.

"Yes! I can hardly wait for the Atlanta trip. Maybe we're both dummies. Do you understand what I'm saying? We have a lot to talk about."

"Yes, we do," he agreed. After a slight pause, he added, "You're so bright. You're so wise. And, you're so much better at this than I."

Carley laughed, a beautiful and deep and unrestrained laugh.

* * *

Patten met with Carley on Thursday and Friday mornings to check the weather and review her cross-country planning. He was tense while she was gone both days. When not with a student, he could not relax: he was in a negative mood, pacing the floor and ramp and making numerous calls for updated weather reports. Linda once asked suspiciously if something was wrong. A scowl froze any other questions she might have been tempted to ask.

He was especially edgy on Friday. The weather reports had been iffy with a fifty percent chance of thunderstorms along her route on the return trip. He told her he didn't want to sign her off for the trip. But when she asked him if he would sign off any other student for the trip with the same weather forecast, he had to admit that he would. She assured him that she would be careful, would check with flight watch frequently for updated weather, and would take refuge at the nearest airport if weather problems developed. After going over with her the various airports along her route of flight, he signed her logbook off for the trip. She was cheerful and confident as he walked with her out to the one fifty-two, and she reassured him again she would obtain radar following and would be fine.

He had a frightening time, though, in the late afternoon before she returned. He was flying with a new student when, looking toward the northwest, he saw menacing, dark, cumulonimbus clouds billowing upward and outward some 20 miles away at about 8,000 feet. Thin strands of virga hung beneath the thunderheads, partially obscuring the horizon.

Patten cut short the new student's lesson and returned to Gulf Shores Aviation. He heard rumbling thunder in the distance. While the student waited, he hurried to his office and called the flight service station. After a few minutes that seemed more like hours, he was told that the one fifty-two was 25 miles northwest of Gulf Shores Aviation, and that other than light green on the radar screen, no significant weather was observed or reported. Patten's nerves settled some after this report—she would be on the ground in about 15 minutes, he calculated.

He finished his chores with the student, rescheduled her, and instructed Linda to inform him when Carley called in for an airport advisory. She did so in five minutes, and Patten was standing on the ramp when the one fifty-two appeared on downwind. He waited as she taxied up to the ramp.

He fought the prop blast and struggled to open her door as she cut the engine.

She was cheerful as she gathered her flight bag and charts and described the trip to him as they walked to the office and into the flight instruction room. He didn't break her good mood by telling her how worried he had been. She had flown through some light sprinkles and mild turbulence, but had radar following all the way and was never afraid. The engine had started running a little rough a few miles out. The application of carburetor heat didn't help, but the engine smoothed out when she turned the switch key to the right magneto position.

"Probably fouled plugs," Patten surmised. "I'll have the mechanic check it out, and I'll show you how to burn the carbon off the plugs the next time we fly together." He was having trouble keeping his hands off her. "You're doing so well, Carley. You follow instructions, fly safely and frequently, and remember emergency procedures—you're just one hell of a fine student!"

"No secret there...look who taught me!" she smiled. Then she became serious. "But did you worry about me, just a little bit, while I was flying?"

"That's like asking the survivors of the Titanic if they were a little disappointed in their cruise!" he chuckled. "But I won't bore you with the depressing details of my...let's say, barely controlled emotional torment."

"I have to go now to pick up Mark," Carley said. "I'm very excited about the Atlanta trip; he is too."

"Then I'll see you tomorrow."

After Carley left, Patten walked out to the hangar and found Chip taking a small engine apart on the workbench. A colorful ultralight airplane rested on its tail near the bench.

Seeing Patten approaching, Chip put down a ratchet wrench and wiped his hands on a grease cloth.

"Hey Patten, how's it going?"

"We have a rough running engine on the one fifty-two. Maybe you could take a look at it when you get a chance."

"Sure. I'll check it out before I go home this afternoon. Look what I have here," Chip said, indicating the engine.

"It's a small engine. What's it off of, a chainsaw?" Patten smiled.

"Oh, come on man! This little honey is a Rotex engine—goes in that ultralight sitting over there." Chip said, nodding toward the bright red and white ultralight.

"A guy showed up this morning and wanted me to service it. He has a small farm, keeps it out in his barn, and uses his pasture for the short runway required of this baby."

"Did you find something wrong with it…looks like you're taking the thing apart?"

"No. I was just interested. I've never worked on a Rotex before. To really understand an engine, you have to get inside it to see what makes it tick," he said, strong emotion evident in his face. "Curiosity, I guess. Anyway, I've taken it apart, sort of experienced it, and now I feel I know it," Chip explained with a bit of embarrassment as well as a sense of satisfaction. "Now I'm putting it back together again."

He pondered for a short time. "I've been like that as far back as I can remember," he continued. "I've always wanted to get inside things to see how they work."

Patten looked at him intently. "Engines all work about the same way, don't they?"

"Generally speaking, yes. But there are some differences from engine to engine," he asserted. "I like to understand those differences."

"Anyway, I'll have it back together in a few minutes," Chip went on. "Then I'll check out the one fifty-two."

"Okay. Let me know if the airplane has to be grounded. The flight instruction schedule is tight," he said.

"I'll leave you a note if you're not here, but say, Patten, that pretty student you have has been running the prop off the one fifty-two!"

"Carley Price?" He smiled and his face brightened. "Yes, she's been flying a lot lately. She wants to get her private pilot license as soon as she can. She's a good student," he added.

"That too, huh?" Chip gave Patten a knowing look. "Hey, I bet you're going to miss her!" he laughed.

Patten flushed. "Yeah, but she's a student—"

"Hey, she's first a woman, and beautiful at that!" Chip countered.

"...and married!"

Chip turned serious. "Hey, don't get me wrong. Lately, I've seen you loosen up some, look as though you're alive, even smile from time to time. I don't know if that woman has anything to do with it, but if she does, I'm thankful."

Patten shrugged. He didn't know what to say. "Well, talk to you later," he finally uttered and walked away.

Chapter Fifteen

He awoke at the end of a dream in which he was flying over Pasadena, California, and desperately needed to land. As he circled, he had a spectacular view of the Parade of Roses. He turned to land at the airport, but saw that the runway was covered with beautiful roses in a variety of colors. In agony, he realized that he could not land without destroying the roses.

After lying in bed a few minutes trying to digest the troubling dream, he showered, dressed, and left the duplex for the airport. The discomfort of the dream waned as he was soon acutely aware of the particularly vivid colors of buildings, signs, grass and trees along the roadway.

And, he was unusually aware of the pleasant and exciting milieu of the airport when he arrived at work. Usually relegated to background noise in his mind, the local flight activity on the PA system he had installed when he first opened for business here came through crisp and clear. A Lear called in for a traffic advisory; a student, already in the air for dual instruction on this bright morning, reported downwind; and a Cessna twin reported departing runway one-eight. The scent of aviation fuel in the air was pleasurably familiar. He stopped on his way across the ramp to admire the picture of speed exuded by a sleek, brightly colored Mooney anchored on the ramp. He felt at home, contented, in a place where he belonged.

Patten was in an upbeat mood when George arrived for his final flight preparation before his FAA check flight with an examiner in Montgomery.

"Hi George, ready for the flight test?"

"Hope so. Guess we'll know today?"

"You'll do fine. We'll go through all the maneuvers today the examiner will put you through on Sunday. First, we'll stay in the traffic pattern and perform the short and soft field takeoffs and landings, forward and side slips, then go to the north practice area for ground reference maneuvers. After that, we'll do the high work. We'll practice instrument work under the hood, and you can expect that I'll simulate an engine out and smoke in the cockpit to check your knowledge of emergency procedures. You'll practice everything today that you'll get on the FAA checkride except for cross-country planning. You've done all these things before—just never bunched up back-to-back as they will be today and again tomorrow for the checkride.

"Remember, always use the checklist—don't trust your memory. Even if your memory is impeccable, the examiner requires use of the checklist."

The flight went well. Patten had to correct George on approach to landing stalls because the student tended to lose too much altitude. All in all, Patten was certain that George would pass the checkride. Now and then he thought himself very lucky that he had such competent flight instructors and students; he felt proud of all of them, especially so today, as he watched George perform, undaunted, and with the confidence that comes from knowledge and skill, every task put before him. He knew that Carley would do as well.

By the time Patten had signed George's logbook and wrote in the authorization for the checkride, he was beginning to worry again about Carley and the trip to Atlanta. He had a foreboding of things going sour. He knew the potential for pain—his, and even worse, Carley's. However strong the temptation, he knew he could not knowingly break up a family and live with himself.

He found Carley's number in her file and telephoned her.

"Carley, this is Patten—"

She broke in, "Mr. Fortis?"

'Mr. Fortis' now sounded strange to Patten. He had to chuckle. He could no longer hide behind a formality. "I think 'Patten' is more appropriate at this point, don't you? Listen, Carley, I'm sorry to be so indecisive, but I don't know if going to Atlanta with you is such a good idea. You're married, and I don't want to do anything to break up your home. I have many problems. In fact, I've mostly avoided relationships for a long time. If you knew me, I don't think you would want to get involved."

She sounded relaxed and earnest, "Patten, there *is* a lot we don't know about each other. As for me being married...I guess I am. But I don't see and rarely hear from Jack more than once or twice a year. Mark and I are not important to him. Mark wouldn't know what his father looks like if I didn't keep pictures out." She now wept softly. "I'm lonely; I need to feel important to someone! I usually don't know if Jack is alive or dead. He doesn't want me to try and find him. He doesn't want me to bother him. Oh, it's a long story...when we have more time to talk, I'll tell you about it." She paused for a moment, and he could hear her blotting her eyes. "I...uh...told my mother-in-law you were going to Atlanta and that Mark and I would fly with you. So everything is okay with that—I mean, I don't have to hide that, do you understand?

"As for your problems, well, you're not unique, you know. I'll tell you sometime about how low I was when I first met you. Yet today, I feel good again. I'm alive. I'm happy. I've been packing and having fun. I do think that we should go slowly and get to know each other. Oh, and Mark is looking forward to flying. But I guess I should ask: Do you like kids?"

Memories of rolling around on the lawn, playing with Steve when he was a preschool child, flashed through Patten's mind. "I love kids," he said seriously.

"If you don't want to go with us, I'll go ahead and drive."

"No, I really want to go with you," Patten said. "I just don't want to hurt you, or to hurt myself. I've been through some tough times and didn't handle them well. I've been…well, scared, and avoided relationships," he told her again.

"Thanks for thinking about my feelings," she replied. "But I'm a grown woman, and responsible for myself. I'll be okay," she said confidently.

Patten was taken aback and didn't know what to say. He was intrigued, but for some reason unsettled. *Can I turn loose? Release the burden?* Her mind was obviously made up.

She paused for a moment, then went on, "By the way, if you haven't made reservations yet, you might think about staying at the Marriott on Peachtree Northeast. That's close to where my aunt lives. I could borrow her car, and we could have dinner if you like."

"Okay, but look, I don't want to get you in any trouble."

"Thanks, but don't worry about it, Patten. Everything is going to work out. See you at a quarter of seven then."

After Carley hung up, Patten felt energized again. He wished he could be as confident and decisive as Carley sounded. He didn't know how this relationship might turn out, but he was too excited to stew about it anymore.

He called the Marriott and made the reservation, then filed an instrument flight plan direct to Charlie Brown at 11,000 feet. In the weather briefing he learned that a cold front was moving eastwardly across Alabama, and his flight path would take him into stratus clouds and rain before reaching Atlanta. There was a chance of thunderstorms. Ceiling was forecast to be 600 feet in fog and rain at Charlie Brown, so he requested the instrument approach for runway eight.

After flying with his last student of the day, Patten had the four fuel tanks of the Aztec topped off. He then preflighted the airplane, having to crawl on his hands and knees under each wing to sample the fuel for water. Finding no telltale line of separation of fuel and water in the sample cup, he checked the oil in each engine and added a quart of 50-weight to the starboard engine. He inspected the airframe and checked the control surfaces, then entered the cockpit and twisted a valve between the seats to discharge onto the ramp a small amount of fuel along with any contaminants that might have settled in the fuel line. Finally, he prepared the intercom and headsets for himself, Carley, and Mark.

Chapter Sixteen

Patten drove to the duplex, showered and changed clothes. He packed an overnight bag, picked up a sandwich, and was back at the airport by half past six. Linda was gone for the day and the offices were deserted. He called for a weather briefing update, and found no significant change in the enroute or terminal weather.

Hearing a car pull up on gravel, he looked out to the parking lot, and saw that it was Carley and Mark. He hurried outside to help with their luggage.

Carley helped Mark, a hazel-eyed, brown-headed four-year old, out of his seatbelt.

Mark jumped out of the car.

"Mark, say 'hello' to Mr. Fortis. He's teaching me to fly airplanes. He owns this airport."

Patten laughed, as he squatted to meet Mark at eye-level. "Not quite. Hi Mark, good to see you. Ready to take an airplane ride?"

"Yeah. Let's go!" Mark said, racing toward the lobby door.

"As you see, Mark's very excited about the trip," Carley said as she stepped to the rear of the car.

"No more than I," Patten said. "I'll help you with your luggage."

"Mark, help us out with the luggage," Carley called.

Carley opened the trunk, which was stuffed with two suitcases, a small overnight bag, and a long garment bag. "Women don't travel light, you know. Do you think we're going to have to do a new weight and balance on the airplane?" she asked, at once both joking and apologetic.

"We won't have to worry about weight on this trip. One thing they say about the Aztec, Carley, is that if you can close the door on it, the Aztec will fly it. For that reason I hear it's a favorite of drug dealers."

Patten handed a small overnight bag to Mark, who had returned and was throwing gravel across the parking lot. "Think you can handle this one?"

"Yeah!" Mark grabbed the bag and ran back to the office.

"Energetic and enthusiastic, isn't he?" Patten said as he took two of the suitcases and started inside the offices. Carley followed with the garment bag.

"He never slows down. And he's really excited about this trip. He's never flown before."

"He'll enjoy it," Patten surmised. "But the droning of those 500 horses will probably put him to sleep right away once we reach altitude."

"What altitude are we flying?"

"Eleven thousand," he replied. "Atlanta is about 250 nautical miles. We should arrive there in an hour and a half or so. We'll be cruising at around 200 mph. I filed an IFR flight plan," he went on. "We'll be pushing through stratus clouds before we get there, and the ceiling is low. We'll probably make an instrument approach to land. The Aztec has a Loran for navigation, so we'll be able to fly direct. When I get some extra money I'll put a GPS, a global positioning system, in this airplane."

Patten telephoned the Jacksonville flight service station and copied the clearance as Carley showed Mark around the offices.

They loaded the luggage into the baggage compartment of the Aztec, and Patten strapped Mark into his seat. He adjusted Mark's headset as small as it would go, but it was still a poor fit. Patten and Carley belted themselves in.

"Why don't I get us airborne, and then you take over—give you some good multiengine and 'flight in instrument meteorological conditions' experience," Patten suggested.

"Flight into IMC," she smiled.

"Yes, you remembered. But flight into IMC is what you're not supposed to do until you get your instrument ticket!"

"Right! But I have to know about it. I have my written test coming up," she said. "I'm glad you're along. I'd freak out if I were to fly into clouds where I couldn't see anything."

"You've done well flying under the hood. You won't worry at all after you get more practice flying in reference to the flight instruments," he assured her.

Carley looked over the array of switches, gauges, panel instruments, and navigation and communication gear. "How do you keep up with all this?"

"It just takes a little getting used to." Patten quickly went through the prestart checklist and fired up the left engine, followed by the right. He turned on the avionics, and set the Loran for FTY, the identification letters for Brown airport.

He spoke into the intercom: "The Loran makes navigation so easy it's like cheating. The screen will show the distance to our destination—Brown Airport—also groundspeed, estimated time of arrival, course to fly, whether we're flying off course and in which direction, etc. Beats pilotage and dead reckoning, don't you think?"

Carley nodded agreement.

Patten taxied to runway one-eight, and quickly completed the take-off checklist. Darkness was falling as he departed the runway and raised the wheels. Reducing the power to 25 inches manifold pressure and the prop speed to 2,500 RPM, he turned left to a heading of 045 degrees. Switching off the landing light, he called Jacksonville Center, where he was picked up on radar as he climbed through 3,000 feet. At 11,000 feet, he reported reaching the designated altitude, and further reduced power to 23 inches manifold and 2300 rpm prop speed. He spent a few seconds synchronizing the props.

"Climbs a little faster than the one fifty-two, doesn't it? Okay Carley, you have it. Try to maintain 11,000 feet and 045 degrees heading."

Carley gingerly grasped the yoke, being momentarily intimidated by the power of the engines and the large size of the Aztec as compared to that of the Cessna one fifty-two.

Patten looked back. "How are you doing, Mark?"

The headset overpowered Mark's small, thin face, which he had glued against the port side window. "There're lots of lights down there!" he said into the headset, as he turned wide-eyed to look at Patten.

"Looks like he's enjoying the ride," Patten said to Carley. "I don't know if the headset fits him well enough to keep the noise out. Those engines are noisy!"

Carley held the heading within ten degrees and the altitude within 200 feet.

"You're doing fine," Patten smiled at Carley.

"I'm glad *you* think so," she said as she concentrated on the controls and flight instruments.

Twenty minutes out of Gulf Shores Aviation, Patten glanced back at Mark and saw that he was fast asleep with the headset askew, one earpiece resting on his nose. He unplugged Mark from the intercom.

Patten tweaked the rpm on the right engine to again synchronize the props. "I'm afraid your son has turned in for the trip. I disconnected him from the intercom."

Carley turned and looked over her shoulder. She laughed. "Looks like he hasn't a care in the world!"

"I wish I could remember what that's like!" Patten said.

"Me, too," Carley agreed, "but I'm happier now than I remember ever being before." She reached over and put her hand on Patten's knee.

Patten felt contentment at this moment. He felt a closeness, a bond with Carley and Mark, although he had just met Mark.

Jacksonville Center called for One Niner Juliet to switch over to the Montgomery approach frequency, as the Aztec was departing the Jacksonville Center area.

Patten switched frequencies, called Montgomery approach and advised that he was level at 11,000.

He showed Carley on the instrument chart the boundaries area, and where they would likely be switched over to Atlanta Center.

"This is a pleasure trip, isn't it?" Patten wanted to know.

"Yes, I think so." Carley's eyes twinkled.

"We're not flight instructing, are we?"

"Well, no, I guess not."

As they exchanged looks, they became aware only of each other. Patten swiveled his microphone to one side, and moved Carley's mike down away from her mouth. They embraced and kissed.

A voice on the radio brought him back to reality: "Aztec One Niner Juliet, Montgomery approach. Report altitude!"

Patten adjusted his microphone. "One Niner Juliet, climbing back to 11,000. Momentarily off altitude. Over."

"Roger. Montgomery altimeter setting 29.72."

"Roger."

Patten adjusted the altimeter to reflect 29.72 in the Holtzman window. Carley looked a little disturbed. "Guess we'd better wait until we're on the ground," she said.

"I can't wait," Patten said. He set the switches for heading and altitude on the autopilot, made minor adjustments, and turned to Carley. "What do you think autopilots were made for?" he said playfully as he reached over and embraced her again.

They kissed and he was lost in his experience of her again until the radio commanded his attention once more.

"Aztec One Niner Juliet, Aztec One Niner Juliet, Montgomery approach, how do you read, over?"

"One Niner Juliet, loud and clear," Patten responded.

"Aztec One Niner Juliet, Montgomery approach. I've called you several times without response. Answer your radio, please! I can't spend all my time trying to raise you! Over!"

"Aztec One Niner Juliet, roger." Patten and Carley smiled at each other.

"Aztec One Niner Juliet, contact Atlanta on 124.5. Good day!"

Patten gave Carley, who was laughing, a small, yielding grin. "I guess we'll have to keep our mind on flying...though that guy obviously didn't realize we were having an emergency of sorts up here."

He switched over to the Atlanta frequency and reported the altitude.

"This is so beautiful," Carley said softly as she surveyed the earth below. She was fascinated by the kaleidoscope of lights on the ground, which spread west, south and east to the horizon. Twinkling lights below slowly disappeared under the wings as the craft sped on its way. The myriad lights were multicolored; some were blinking, some steady. Looking up, she saw the starlit and so-far moonless sky glittering merrily.

Montgomery was brightly lit behind the left wing. Patten identified Columbus, Georgia for her in the distance, just outboard of the starboard engine.

In contrast, the area ahead, to the northeast, appeared dark and foreboding.

"What's that, at twelve o'clock," Carley asked.

"Stratus," replied Patten. "We'll be in there in a few minutes."

Patten took Carley's hand. He lifted her hand to his lips and kissed and nibbled on her warm fingers, pale and soft in the rosy glow of the cockpit nightlights. They relaxed in their seats, held hands, and enjoyed each other's presence.

The Aztec rolled slightly as it entered the stratus layer, and intermittent, bright, pulsating light flooded the cockpit. Patten snapped a toggle switch on the panel to cut off the strobe lights. In response to a questioning look from Carley, he explained, "The strobes bouncing off the clouds are distracting and wash out night vision." The flashes of strobes off the clouds stopped, and gray murk surrounded the airplane. Soft reflections of the red and green position lights on the wing tips were barely visible from the cockpit. The engines droned on, thrusting the nose of the airplane deeper and deeper into the gray nothingness ahead.

"You have to be a trusting soul to fly inside clouds," Carley mused, "not knowing whether you'll be smashing into the side of a mountain or another airplane in front of you." She was beginning to feel a little uneasy as she explored the possibilities. She squeezed Patten's hand.

"Can't see anything in this soup, all right, so you have to trust the flight instruments, and those controllers on the ground know our altitude and position from our transponder signals—(he tapped the blinking light on the transponder in the panel)—and can see on their radar scopes and report to us any other airplanes that happen to be around. And, the rules of the air require an airplane flying southwest, toward us, to be flying at a different altitude to avoid collision, as you studied already." Patten reassured her.

Carley's anxiety was temporary, and she reached over and embraced Patten again. Surrounded by the amorphous gray mist, she felt a sense of privacy with Patten that she had not had before. There was something about being hidden, having a romance illicit in some ways, and the felt danger of crashing headlong through the clouds that excited her. She pushed her breasts against Patten's tight chest and ran her hands under his collar, massaging the muscles along his shoulders and chest. She became breathless. Her nipples tingled, and she felt wet heat.

Mild turbulence and lines of water streaking off the windscreen caught Patten's attention. "Looks like we're getting into some light rain—nothing severe in the forecast, though. Let's tighten our seat belts and shoulder straps just in case we run into more turbulence." Patten turned up the cockpit lights momentarily, then reached back to Mark and tightened his seatbelt.

Patten saw a hint of fear again in Carley's eyes. "We're all right," he said.

The rain came harder. Large drops struck the airframe and windscreen and now made racket enough to overcome the noise-canceling ability of the headsets. Even the noise of the engines became relegated to background noise. The Aztec suddenly struck a wall of water, and was pushed around in every direction by increasing turbulence. The autopilot worked continuously to hold altitude and heading. Patten pulled both throttles back to maneuvering speed to reduce stress on the airframe.

He quickly glanced back at Mark, who had awakened and was laughing as he was thrown from side to side against the seat belt.

"The autopilot is being overworked." Patten raised his voice on the intercom so he could be heard over the din of the rain. "I'm turning it off. See if you can hold altitude at 11,000 feet. The Loran shows a heading of 080 to get us back on course."

Patten tried to appear relaxed. He wasn't!

Carley had turned whitish and was frozen in her seat for a moment, but then grasped the yoke with both hands and pushed her feet forward to connect with the rudder pedals. "I'll do the best I can!" she shouted.

The turbulence grew stronger as they were caught in the fury of the storm. The hands of the altimeter and airspeed indicator moved up and down wildly. The Aztec rolled and pitched violently while Carley strained against the yoke and rudder pedals trying to hold it straight and level. "I can't control it!" she shouted.

Patten lowered the wheels. "They'll help to stabilize the airplane," he responded loudly to her inquiring look.

Sheets of rain pelted the airplane, causing a deafening roar between bursts of thunder. Patten looked back at Mark, who was no longer laughing, but was frightened. Patten reached back and pressed his knee. Trying to calm him down with words was useless, as they would not be heard above the din.

The Aztec careened through the raging storm. Blinding flashes of sheet lightening illuminated a frightening picture of the airplane plowing through the heavy rain. Violent wind shear alternately slammed them down in their seats and threw them upward until the seatbelts and shoulder straps cut into their shoulders, laps and chests. Powerful air currents created strong and sudden yaws that penned them against the cockpit walls and then threw them in the opposite direction as far as the seat belts and shoulder harnesses allowed.

"Just watch the turn and bank indicator to keep the wings level—don't worry so much about the heading or altitude!" he shouted as the torrents of rain now mixed with balls of hail pounded the airframe.

A bolt of lightning abruptly slashed across the sky, and an explosion of thunder pierced their eardrums and sent a tremor through the airframe. The cockpit lights and instrument panel lights immediately went black. The cockpit was shrouded in darkness for a few seconds until Patten switched on the red beam of the emergency flashlight he had taken from his flight bag.

"Hold the yoke and rudder as steady as you can for a moment," he shouted. "Don't look at the turn and bank: it's electrical and has stopped working!"

"I'll try!"

Because of the turbulence, Patten had difficulty controlling his hand to feel along the bank of circuit breakers, but eventually found the ones that had popped out, and hurriedly pushed them back in.

The lights on the instrument panel and the red glow of the cockpit night light returned. Patten shouted, "Okay. You can use the turn and bank again. Keep the wings as level as you can!"

Patten keyed his microphone, "Atlanta center, Aztec One Niner Juliet. Encountered heavy rain, hail, and moderate to severe turbulence. Request altitude range 9,000 to 13,000, over." He couldn't understand center's response over the noise.

He tried several times before he was successful in grasping the volume control knob of the radio on the shaking airplane. Finally, he managed to turn the volume up so that he could hear over the noise of the rain, hail and thunder. "Center, Aztec One Niner Juliet. Say again. Over."

"One Niner Juliet, Atlanta. You are cleared for an altitude block 9,000 to 13,000 feet until further notice. Radar shows you in an area of heavy precip that extends about five miles ahead of you, an embedded thunderstorm that just developed—wasn't there a few minutes ago."

"One Niner Juliet, roger, understand cleared for 9 to 13,000?"

"That's affirmative."

Patten turned to Carley. "You're doing okay. We're in a thunderstorm but should be through it in three minutes!" he shouted.

Carley was wild-eyed, but wrestled with the yoke and strained on the rudder to right the airplane as first one and then the other wing was thrust upward then downward by the turbulence. She strained to pull the nose up in the downdrafts and to push the nose down in the updrafts, and tried to control the yawing with the rudder. Her eyes were glued on the turn and bank indicator. Beads of perspiration lined her forehead and nose. In a strained voice she shouted at Patten, "You take it!"

He thought for a second, and then said as calmly as he could, "You're doing as well as I could. We'll be okay and be out of this in a minute!"

But Patten wasn't all that confident. Guilt suddenly overwhelmed him. *They trust and depend on me, and I've put them in danger! Light airplanes aren't built to withstand the forces of severe turbulence in thunderstorms—even airliners can and have broken up.*

Patten put his hand on Carley's shoulder and yelled louder: "We'll be out of this thunderstorm shortly. Level the wings and try to keep the altitude between nine and thirteen thousand!"

Then, as swiftly as it had started, both turbulence and rain ceased. The noise diminished, and except for an occasional wobble, the Aztec was stable. Carley was wet with perspiration, but the tension disappeared from her face.

"We're out of it!" Patten said. "Good job!" He loosened his seatbelt and smiled at Carley while reaching back to loosen Mark's seatbelt. He plugged Mark's headset back into the intercom. "Your mom did a good job of flying through the storm, Mark."

Beaming, Mark reached in front of him and patted Carley on the shoulder.

Carley smiled with relief and contentment.

"I'm certainly glad you were here," she said.

"I wouldn't have missed it," he replied as he stroked her cheek. "Now that you've done all the work, I'll take over and give you a rest."

Flight instruments gradually stopped tumbling. After setting the directional gyroscope to agree with the now calm compass, they noted they were seventy degrees west of course. The altimeter read 9,500 feet.

"One Niner Juliet, Atlanta. Radar shows you out of the heavy precip."

Patten turned the volume back down on the radio. "One Niner Juliet, that's affirmative. Making a climbing right turn back on course to 11,000." Patten pushed the throttles to climb power and raised the wheels.

"Roger. Report reaching 11,000."

After reaching assigned altitude, Patten returned to cruise power and again set the autopilot. The rain stopped completely, and the Aztec glided smoothly through the stratus clouds on course, according to the Loran display.

"Atlanta Center, One Niner Juliet, level at eleven."

"Roger, One Niner Juliet."

He turned to Carley. "The Loran shows we have only 25 miles to go to reach Charlie Brown," Patten reported. "We'll start our descent shortly."

Carley laughed. "I can't get used to the name of the airport. Mark will think Snoopy is waiting!"

"That's bad!" Patten said.

"I want to see Snoopy," Mark said.

"See what you started," Carley feigned anger.

"Who started?" Patten asked.

"Are we having our first fight?" Carley smiled.

"Not likely to be our last," Patten predicted. "Sorry Mark, but there's no Snoopy at this airport."

"Oh, no!" Mark said, but he didn't seem all that disappointed.

Ten minutes later, they were radar-vectored to the instrument landing beam, dropped the wheels, and followed the visually presented radio signals to align with and descend toward the runway. They broke out of the clouds at 500 feet. Switching frequencies to Brown tower, they landed and was guided to the FBO by ground control. As soon as the Aztec was secured, they took their luggage and called the Marriott for transportation.

Chapter Seventeen

While Carley was gone to her aunt's with Mark, Patten found a florist across the street and purchased a dozen roses. A search of a liquor store on the next block yielded a bottle of Bailey's Irish Crème.

He returned to his room to await Carley. The clock was nearing nine when the telephone rang.

Carley was breathless: "I'm downstairs. Sorry I took so long…had to freshen up a bit…flying in a thunderstorm is hard work!"

"I'm just now ready myself. And starved," he added. "Could you come by the room a minute, though, before we go to eat?"

"Is it safe?" she teased.

"No guarantees," he laughingly replied.

"You're the one who may not be safe!" she warned.

He answered her knock at the door shortly and was awestruck: her beauty was arresting. She had changed into a red cocktail dress, matching heels and purse. She searched his face for signs of approval.

He handed her the bouquet of roses.

"Oh, they're so beautiful!" she exclaimed, with moist eyes.

"Carley, you…are stunning. Compared to you, they're nothing."

In the open doorway, he hugged her and gently kissed her forehead. "We ought to go eat now."

"Yes, we should. Thank you so much for the roses. Can I leave them here until after we eat?"

His pulse quickened. "Of course," he replied, as he took the bouquet and placed it on the dresser. "You know the city. Why don't you choose the restaurant?"

"I enjoy the vegetarian dishes at Café Sunflower, but they close at 9:30. Do you like Italian?"

"Yes, it's great."

As they were walking down the hall, Carley dug in her purse and came up with car keys, which she handed to Patten.

"You pilot, I'll navigate," she said.

"That's a change! But it's not fair. You only had to fly through a thunderstorm. I have to deal with the Peachtree traffic!" he protested.

"I know you can do it," she smiled.

"Touché!"

They wound their way north through the traffic to Stephano's, a restaurant in an unassuming square building near the street and fronted by a small and full parking lot. Inside, however, the restaurant was tastefully decorated, and the most was made of the available space by the ingenious placing of plants and dividers that created an air of privacy at each table.

After a short wait, an Italian-looking waiter led Patten and Carley to a semi-circular table in the center of the restaurant. They ordered wine and mulled over the menu. They were holding hands underneath the table and looking into each other's eyes oblivious to the waiter who was now asking a second time if they were ready to order.

The shuffling of the waiter standing next to them caught Patten's attention, and he clumsily placed their orders.

As the waiter left the table, Patten and Carley grinned sheepishly at each other.

"This is embarrassing," Carley said. "Everyone is looking at us!"

"They're looking at the most beautiful woman they've ever seen."

"Oh, you!" Carley pretended to be miffed.

As they were eating, Carley said: "Why did you not take the controls in the thunderstorm?" she asked.

He recalled that he had the impulse to do just that. "You've had training on instruments already, under the hood…"

"Yes, but not in turbulence like *that*! I was way off course and altitude!"

"Look Carley, in that weather I would have been off course and altitude also. In fact, a strong horizontal or vertical wind shear could have damaged the control surfaces of the airplane if we had tried too hard to maintain course and altitude!"

"I was scared!"

"So was I. But it will help you to remember the three rules of flying in thunderstorms, the ones you learned in ground school."

Carley laughed: "One, stay out of thunderstorms; two, stay out of thunderstorms; and three, stay out of thunderstorms!"

"Since you actually flew in a thunderstorm, I don't think you're likely to forget those rules!"

Carley paused and locked onto his eyes. "I want to kiss you."

"I *want* you to kiss me."

"Let's go."

They bolted toward the exit, almost overturning the table. Halfway out, Carley grabbed Patten's arm. "The check!"

"What?"

"The check, we forgot to pay!"

Their waiter spotted them and hurried over. "Are you ready to leave? Was the food good?"

"Yes, the food was excellent," Patten said. "Could I have the check?"

"But you haven't had the tira misu…but one moment." The waiter hurried off and soon returned with the check.

"Thanks." Patten rushed off to the cashier. Having paid the bill, Patten and Carley again headed for the exit, but once again Carley squeezed Patten's arm. "The tip!"

Patten dutifully returned to the table and left a tip.

He challenged the traffic on the way back to the Marriott, weaving in and out and using all lanes going in his direction.

After she cautioned him a second time, Carley laughed, "This is not the Talladega Speedway. Let's get back to the safety of the thunderstorm!"

"Oh, sorry. I'm preoccupied."

"About what?"

"You, of course."

She smiled. "I'm glad you're thinking of me."

They pulled into the Marriott parking lot, hurriedly made it to the elevator, and walked quickly through the hall to his room. Once inside, he embraced her.

"I'm ready for that kiss."

She kissed him long and hard, pressing her body against his.

"I hope you don't have to get back to your aunt's soon."

"No. She told me to stay out as long as I wanted—not to worry about Mark. I think she's happy to have Mark alone with her. But I do want to call and check on him."

While Carley telephoned, Patten poured each a drink of Bailey's.

"Everything okay?" he asked, as he handed her a drink.

"Yes, Mark is asleep and my aunt is going to bed. I have a house key and won't have to disturb her when I get in."

"Good. Let's talk," he said, as he pulled out a chair for her on one side of the coffee table and he sat on the other side.

"You're distancing yourself from me," Carley said, as she mocked a pout.

"It's the only way I can think. When I'm close to you, my mind goes blank! I become utterly incompetent, as in the restaurant, and driving on Peachtree. It's amazing! But we need to talk. I don't want this to wind up bad for you."

"Do you always worry so much? I don't want to be hurt either, and I don't want you to be, but…"

"Tell me about your marriage, Carley. What did you mean when you said that you were but you weren't? You can't be halfway married, unless you mean you're separated."

Carley laughed, and then her eyes turned sad. "Separated is accurate! I'm married but I haven't seen Jack in two years. I haven't heard from him in six months. I don't know if he's alive or dead. Am I making any sense?"

"He likes to travel," she continued. "He's with, or was with, a construction outfit in the Middle East, repairing oil wells, or something."

"Doesn't he call? Can't you call him?"

"He doesn't call, and he becomes angry if I try to contact him. He doesn't want me to bother him. Each month funds show up in my checking account." She was thoughtful for a moment. "If he were dead, I don't think he would continue to be paid, do you?"

"No, I don't think so."

"He never had any interest in writing or calling, even on birthdays, anniversaries, or holidays. His mother always makes excuses for him.

"But, his mother is a wonderful person. She's been a big help in raising Mark. She loves Mark, and, I think, needs him to make her life more meaningful. You can understand what she's going through: her husband died three years ago, and now her only child, Jack, stays away and doesn't want to be disturbed. She told me she considered herself lucky to have a daughter-in-law who denied jealous, territorial instincts in herself in order to make life more satisfying and full for her children, husband, and in-laws, and who had been generous and kind in allowing and even encouraging her and Mark to cultivate a bond. She has done what she can to make life easier for me and for Mark, and I'm sure she feels ashamed that her son is not a better father and husband. She has been more of a mother to me than my own mother.

"But I feel so sorry for Mark. To him, his father is more of an idea—a picture on a mantle—than a person. He's five years old and probably hasn't spent more than two weeks total with him," Carley said, anger now pressuring her voice.

"My father died suddenly of a heart attack when Mark was one year old, and Jack's father died soon after. They both loved Mark, but both passed away, so Mark has no father around and no grandfathers."

Patten was beginning to fathom the depth of Carley's situation. "You've had a rough time. No husband around for that long…and really not knowing whether you had a husband. You must have been very lonely…?"

"Very much so," Carley resumed. "I look around and see couples shopping together, families going on picnics, seeing romantic movies on television…and I feel so depressed. Other people seem to have normal lives, but not me! I guess I've felt sorry for myself for a long time."

Patten knew those feelings. He felt closer to her than ever, and wanted to embrace and comfort her, but restrained himself.

"With good reason! You're too young and beautiful to be alone. You must have had your share of male attention?"

She smiled shyly. "Thanks. I did think about it…but I didn't know what to do. I was married. I wasn't free. And, I didn't really feel attractive; I felt rejected. My husband obviously didn't want to be with me. He doesn't know my birthdate, Mark's birthday, or the date of our anniversary. That's really how little he thinks of me, and of Mark. I didn't think other men would find me attractive either, since he obviously didn't. I just withdrew and stayed at home. After a couple of years of virtual isolation I became frightened even to go out." She paused for a moment, and blotted the silent tears from her eyes.

"I haven't been with any other man, Patten," she continued. "My parents divorced when I was twelve years old, after Dad found that mother was having an affair. I went to live with my father, and I always blamed my mother for his pain and my pain, the breakup of the family, and even his unhappiness afterwards. I swore I would never put my husband and children through that. Do you understand?"

"Yes, you might be surprised how much I understand. But what about this…us?"

She dabbed at her eyes with a tissue. "I'm sorry," she said, "for getting upset."

"Don't be."

"I believe I started turning loose of that part of my past a short time after starting flight training," she continued thoughtfully. "You see, as long as I was afraid, I would have to stay in my situation with Jack. To face my fear of flying, well, I think that was like facing my problems, and learning to get over them, and then to get on with my life. And getting on with my life means no Jack in it. After all, I keep telling myself, I'm not my mother. I'm not responsible for mother's and dad's problems. I'm me! I don't want to hurt anyone, including Jack, but I've learned that I'm responsible for my own life and happiness. Do you know what I'm saying?"

"Yes, I believe so."

"If Jack and I ever did have anything together, it's dead. Sometimes I think he married me to have me live close to his parents to watch after them while he travels!"

Patten lifted her from the chair and carried her to the couch. He held her in his lap and nestled her head on his chest, momentarily overcome with strong nurturing feelings toward her as she sobbed uncontrollably for several minutes. Patten held her tightly and kissed her forehead, her eyelids, her cheeks, and her hair. She relaxed against his chest. Her small arms encircled him, and she squeezed his head down toward her. He was surprised at her strength.

She smothered his face with kisses, then pushed him back slightly and smiled. "Bet you don't think I'm so beautiful now, huh?"

He surveyed her face: her mascara and eye shadow had run in tiny rivulets down her cheeks and dried, and smudges of the black oozed out the corners of her eyes. Her hair was disheveled. Lipstick was smeared an inch around her lips. Suddenly reminded of the gaudy makeup of a clown face, he began to chuckle, then laugh. His laughter became stronger, and he shook all over.

"Should I be hurt or what?" She looked at him quizzically, although with a smile. But Patten's laughter was contagious, and a fit of laughter overcame her.

They both laughed until tears were streaming down their faces. In a few minutes their tension subsided with the fits of laughter.

"Do...I look that awful?" Carley finally managed to say.

"No...not awful, but awfully funny with your makeup all over your face," Patten said.

Carley jumped up and ran to the bathroom. "Oh, how terrible!" she exclaimed as she looked in the mirror. She grabbed a washcloth and began washing her face.

"Carley?"

"Yes?"

"Don't put your makeup back on."

"But I look so awful without it."

"You're gorgeous with or without it. Come and sit by me." He refilled their glasses as she returned to the couch. He kissed her fingers and gently nibbled on her knuckles. He was acutely aware of her breasts as they rose and fell with each breath she took.

He had wanted her continuously since they had been at the restaurant. He ached. "Oh Carley, I want you so much it hurts!" He kissed her, and she returned his kiss passionately, running her hot hand inside his shirt and caressing his chest.

Her passion startled him, and he backed away. He stood up and paced the floor. "Maybe we can talk this thing to death," he said, desperate.

"I don't want to talk it to death," Carley replied, only momentarily subdued. "Why destroy something that makes me feel so good."

"I want you more than anything, Carley, but..."

"But what? What's wrong?"

"Well...I..." Patten stumbled for the right words. "I'm so afraid I'm going to hurt you. You've never done anything like this before. It's been important to you to be faithful in your marriage. You may feel guilty afterwards, and then I would be the cause of your pain. I have a hard time living with myself, anyway, sometimes."

He paused for a moment as he regarded Carley, who looked at him thoughtfully. "And, there are some other things, too."

"Like what?"

"Well, there's an age gap here, for instance," Patten said.

Carley looked hurt. "You think I'm too young and foolish for you!"

He grinned. "Come on, I'm too old for you."

Carley relaxed and smiled. "And just how old are you?"

"Let's just say my birth certificate was found among the Dead Sea scrolls," he laughed.

Carley laughed. "You're not going to say you're old enough to be my…!?"

"Well?"

"You're *not* going to say it!"

"I don't want to be trite, but…"

"Well, just how old are you?"

"I'm 45, and sometimes feel 100!"

"I have no problem with that. I don't really care if you're 79. We're both old enough to make our own decisions."

He looked at her thoughtfully, and then grinned. "I've heard that a woman can spot a man 50 IQ points and 10 years and she's still his equal," Patten said wryly. "That's probably true!"

"I don't know about that. Sometimes I feel so stupid."

"Sometimes you seem so wise. And you seem to handle this—us—much better than I."

Carley smiled, but then turned serious: "What did you mean when you said you had a hard time living with yourself?"

Images of two funerals, and the hostile, blaming face of a plaintiff's attorney and parents who lost their only child raced through Patten's mind, and he unconsciously winced. "I've hurt people in the past, and I don't want it to happen to you," he said.

"You mean you've had many romantic relationships that didn't work out?"

"Oh, no," he had to smile. "For a person my age I've had few romances. I was married once. After the divorce, I changed my life, tried to keep to myself, and threw myself into my work, sort of existing on a day-to-day basis. Defensive, I think I'm learning, but the best way to avoid pain was to avoid involvement, or so I thought."

"I see. A lonely existence, I guess, like mine. But do you want to tell me about the divorce, what caused it?"

Patten sat down on the bed. "There were things that happened, things that turned sour. I was in a position that made me responsible. But the divorce, itself, was probably caused by my depression. I think my wife needed me, and I wasn't able to help her. I let her down. She filed for a divorce, and I didn't protest. I gave her all the property she asked for, and she asked for most of it. I had enough to get a start in aviation, and that's all I wanted."

"Maybe *you* needed but she couldn't give," Carley suggested.

"What? What did you say?"

"Maybe your wife let *you* down."

He was confused for a time. "Let me down? It was my fault, my responsibility. I was supposed to take care of things." He turned pensive. "Or, thought I was..."

"Do you keep in contact with her?"

"No, I haven't talked to her since the divorce, and she's made no effort to contact me. We were never really attached to each other," Patten shrugged.

"I think you understand, though," he said, "that I want to protect you from me, and talking this attraction we apparently have for each other to death may be best, for you as well as for me. But," he sighed, "you know that's not what I want."

"Don't worry about me, Patten. I believe I'm grown-up. I'm stronger now. And I don't know of anything worthwhile without risk."

"If you were hurt, I'd feel responsible."

She looked at him and a smile slowly crept over her face. "I guess I can understand why you feel responsible for me as a student pilot, and I admit a certain feeling of security having you feel responsible for my mistakes and bad feelings—God knows, I wish Jack would care a little about my feelings—but don't do that! Among other things, I want to be a comfort to you, not a burden. You may have had too much of that kind of relationship already."

He was perplexed, as associations raced through his mind. "Well, I don't know what to say."

"Don't say anything. I hope you'll feel relief that you don't have to worry so much about my feelings!" She laughed, "Well, I do want you to worry about my feelings a little, otherwise you wouldn't care about me, would you?"

He smiled, but was excited with associations jumbling up his mind. "You're not likely to suffer any deprivation of care while you're around me!" He paused for a moment. "You're wise beyond your years, beautiful woman," he said.

"Thanks," she said. "I don't feel wise, but I've learned some things about myself that might apply to you, too, things that others have helped me see. Maybe that is a type of wisdom, although I warn you that I can also be very immature and stupid!"

"Come on!"

She laughed. "If you're around me very long, you'll find out!" she said, then more seriously: "What made you so depressed, by the way?"

"It's not pretty." He was silent a short time. "You're pretty! Right now I don't want to talk anymore—I want to hold you." He took her in his arms and kissed her.

"Yes, we can wait on that," she said as she eagerly hugged him tightly.

As they embraced each other, Patten's senses were fine-tuned. He was aware of the delicate, slightly perfumed aroma of her hair, her body pressed against his, and his breathing became irregular and shallow. He moved his head to face her, and ran the tips of his fingers along her forehead, her cheeks, her earlobes, and touched her full, warm lips. Cradling her head in his hands, with his fingers he found the recession at the top of her neck and gently massaged the back of her head. The warmth and texture of her hair was sensuous to his touch. Her face, flushed and slack, was tilted back, and he kissed her eyelids, her cheeks and forehead, and brushed his lips slightly against her lips. As he did so, she moved her tongue tentatively along his lips and inside his mouth. They kissed passionately, eagerly. Patten's body tingled and he felt unbalanced, as Carley went limp in his arms.

He stepped back and their eyes met. They understood that they were one, and were eager to share their bodies with each other. Patten felt a joy and contentment he couldn't remember feeling before.

They abandoned all restraint as they hurriedly removed their clothes. Passion overcame their initial shyness, and eagerness hurried them along. Patten had thought that clothes were worn to hide defects of the body, but saw that she was even more beautiful without clothes: her long well-sculptured legs, firm breasts with taut nipples, tight stomach, and shapely hips were all more than he could ever want. He caressed and kissed her nipples, and her fingernails bit into his shoulders. He entered her, and they quickly climaxed. Her orgiastic spasms pushed him out of her. He penetrated her again, and she moaned with pleasure. They both reached a climax again.

Afterwards they lay close and held each other, momentarily content with each other and the world.

Soon he pulled her face to his and kissed her gently. Her soft, warm lips again awakened the yearning deep inside him and they made love once more.

They spent the night talking and making love. "I think we're making up for a long period of wanting each other," said Carley.

"I think you're right, honey, and we're not through yet, are we?"

"I hope not," she said as she pulled him close. She ran her fingers across his lips, and smiled. "We've kissed so much our lips are chapped!"

"So they are," he said as he kissed her tenderly again.

It was five o'clock when Carley and Patten showered and dressed. Neither wanted to sleep, so they found an all-night diner and had breakfast.

She spoke softly across the table: "How many times did we make love, you think?"

He grinned. "You mean you didn't keep count…again?"

"Oh, you!"

She took a small mirror out of her purse. "I look terrible with no sleep."

"You look great to me," he replied.

"When have you had your eyes examined, pilot?" she asked, a gleam in her eye.

"Airline transport pilot, flight physical every six months, as you so correctly answered in ground school, hon."

"Then you must be looking through rose-colored glasses, dear. Keep them on, please."

"You look beautiful through any kind of eyeglasses, Carley. And I want you to know another fact: I've enjoyed our talk and lovemaking, but I'm beginning to feel sad already; I suppose I'm anticipating parting from you when we fly back to Gulf Shores."

"Hmmm, I had little feelings of depression, too. And it certainly has nothing to do with our relationship. I've enjoyed being with you and have been happier than I've ever been, I think. You've explained my feelings, too. I think I'm leaping ahead to the time we separate when we get back. Isn't that silly! Let's just enjoy this remaining time together. When we do return home, well, we live only a few miles from each other," she said, as much to reassure herself as to comfort Patten.

"That's true, hon, but all the same I miss you already," Patten replied somberly as he looked into her eyes and connected with her soul.

Her eyes were moist. "I've gone from rags to riches," she whispered across the table. "Jack was never very interested in me. We didn't make love even on our wedding night. I thought I must be ugly, or something, but you...you seem to really desire me, and like me."

"Understatement of the century, hon."

Carley blotted tears from her cheeks. "You understand the tears, don't you? You've made me so happy."

"Something is seriously wrong with Jack, hon, that makes him unable to appreciate you."

"I thought something was wrong with me," she sobbed quietly.

He wanted to hold her. "Believe me, the problem is with him."

"You don't know how much you've helped."

"And you've helped me. We should be going now, though. I hope we can see each other again soon when we get back so we can talk more."

"Could we? I know you're busy most of the time."

"Everything will take a backseat to you, hon!"

She smiled. "You think? I don't want to be a pest."

"I'll be the pest, I think."

Back at the Marriott Patten packed up and checked out. He waited in the lobby until a taxicab pulled up with Carley and Mark. Entering the taxi, he spoke to Mark as he placed his hand on the child's shoulder, and instructed the driver to take them to Brown Airport. He enjoyed the feeling of togetherness with Carley and Mark.

Chapter Eighteen

After the students trailed in and took their seats, Patten covered the weather information the students needed to know in order to pass the FAA private pilot written test, but could hardly keep his eyes and mind off Carley. She had her mind on him, too, and the other female students in the class.

Carley stayed after the other students left the ground instruction class. Patten locked the door and they sat close on the couch, embracing. Carley buried her face in Patten's chest. "I hate to admit this, Patten, but I can't bear to even think about you and another woman. I saw all those pretty young girls in your class tonight; I know they'd like to get their hands on you. I'm jealous of you even talking to another woman, especially sitting next to another woman in that one fifty-two. I know it's sick, sick, sick but I hate all your female students! What's wrong with me? I've never been this way before. I don't know if I can tolerate your job!" she exclaimed, feeling weak and helpless.

Patten chuckled.

"You're laughing at me," Carley said, with a hint of anger. "You think I'm so stupid."

He continued to smile. "Not at all. I'm delighted you think I'm so valuable...hope that means you think I'm special. I've heard a saying: If there's no jealousy, there's no caring, at least not romantic caring."

"But it's crazy. It *is* crazy. It's my problem, not yours. I'd absolutely die to see you with another woman, but at the same time I want you to be happy. Does that make any sense?"

"I'd feel the same way," Patten consoled her while at the same time trying to be honest. "I think I'd have a tougher time than you. I don't allow myself to think of you and Jack together," he recoiled at the thought. "I couldn't handle it.

"I'll turn my female students over to another flight instructor if they disturb you. They don't mean anything to me, and there're plenty of male students to keep me busy."

"No!" Carley was adamant. "It shouldn't bother me. I'm crazy. I've got to get over it. You're doing nothing wrong."

"You're not crazy! Or, if you are, I am too," he was just as unwavering. "Anyway, there's no problem giving them up. You would do the same for me."

"No, don't. I'll learn to handle this. I'm not a baby!"

"Okay. But let me know if you want me to make a change. Deal?"

"Deal."

"Carley, let's go ahead and get you ready to take your written and flight tests. Can you fly an hour tomorrow, and maybe a couple of hours the following day? You could be ready for your test this weekend."

Carley pulled his head down and kissed him. "I'd rather do this," she sighed pleasurably.

"I'm game, baby, but...well...we'll have time for other things besides flying in the next few days, I hope."

"If you promise," she moaned softly. "When?"

"When what?" he smiled.

"When can we do the other things besides flying?"

"All the time we're not flying, hon."

"Flying is wonderful," she whispered softly, "but you have to pay some attention to the airplane when you're flying."

"I'm afraid so," he laughed.

Patten gently straightened her up, went behind the counter and returned with the schedule book.

"Tomorrow, ten o'clock meet with your approval?"

"I can't tomorrow morning, but can tomorrow afternoon. Do you have some time in the afternoon?"

"I have a charter flight tomorrow. Why don't you take your written test tomorrow morning? I know you're ready and I'll go ahead and sign you off. Then, why don't we fly the next morning, nine till eleven to get you ready for the flight test?"

"I can make that. Where are you going on the charter flight, dear, and are there going to be any beautiful women on the flight?" Carley asked, only half-kidding.

"Only one, if *you* can go," he said.

"Oh, you're so sweet! Could I?" she said enthusiastically.

"Yes, there's room for you in the copilot's seat if you can go tomorrow afternoon. Destination is Austin, Texas in a King Air. We're leaving at one o'clock and returning at nine or ten in the evening. Can you make it?"

"I think so. If I can get Mark taken care of...his grandmother loves to keep him...I'll be here at one. What should I wear? Whom are you taking to Austin?" she asked excitedly.

"Good! You take the written test tomorrow morning, and we'll schedule the flight test in a couple of weeks," he said. "For the Austin trip, dress casually. Three businessmen are going, and they'll wear business suits. Their tough luck, right?"

"You're so nice to invite me," Carley said as she hugged and kissed him.

"Nothing nice about it, Carley. It's pure selfishness. Really, I'm having a tough time being away from you, even for a little while," he said, seriously.

"You've made me so happy, darling. I had nothing before I met you. Now I have more attention than I've had in my life, more caring than I've ever had, more excitement, friendship, and understanding. I could go on and on! I'm a very lucky woman," she said, while holding him tightly.

"You're very special to me, Carley. I don't want to let you out of my sight: I'm afraid I'll lose you," he said, holding her just as tightly.

* * *

"Don't leave without me!" Carley was excited when she called Patten the following noon. "I'll be there by one. I made 92 on the written test. Am I good or what?"

"I knew you'd have no trouble. Congrats! See you in a few."

Carley liked the luxury of the King Air, the speed, and the altitude at which they could fly in the pressurized cabin with turbo props that Patten explained were just as efficient at twenty thousand feet as at ten thousand feet. Carley and Patten talked little on the flight, as he was busy with piloting. Upon landing at Austin, the businessmen were met by associates at the airport.

"Hon, we don't have to be back here until 6:45. Let's go somewhere to talk and eat," Patten suggested.

"I've never been to Austin before. Do you know a place?"

"There is a place I like to go when I'm here. I hope you like spicy, Cajun seafood or Creole casserole. Would you enjoy that?"

"I'm not hard to please, Patten. I do like spicy seafood. As long as I'm with you, I really don't care where we are or what we eat," she said, squeezing his hand.

They took a taxi to Pappadeaux's on I-35 north, holding hands all the way.

As they ate, the university town milieu brought memories back to Carley of her days at the University of Georgia. Patten asked about her university life. She explained she was a business major, and met Jack while she was a student. Jack worked for a highway construction company. There wasn't much money, and she was torn between returning to Atlanta to take care of her chronically ill father and finishing up college. Her father insisted that she stay at the University.

"Your father loved you," Patten said.

"Yes, he did," Carley said teary-eyed, "and mother broke his heart. I visited her every now and then. We never got along well, mother and me. She told me I was stupid, that she never understood what I meant about anything. I would have to repeat whatever I said to her. She said I never made any sense. Jack, too—he doesn't understand me and thinks I'm stupid."

"Maybe I shouldn't have brought you here. You're reminded of some bad memories."

"No, darling, it's okay. I don't dwell on those bad times anymore, or those more recent, for that matter. I want to think about them, though, to put them in their place. Do you understand? I have you now. That was Carley then. It's almost as though I'm burying her, the unhappy Carley. I cry for her; I feel sorry for her. I know I must sound stupid. But do you understand? It's like grieving for an old friend, someone you knew very well. Does that make any sense?"

He was quiet for a moment as he pondered Patten of old. "That makes good sense to me, Carley. It's tough to give up a part of yourself, someone you've known so long. I guess it's a set of feelings, attitudes about yourself and others, your history, who you really are or were, how you act and react in given circumstances. Even if the old you were miserable, it was nevertheless familiar. It was you! It's difficult to walk away from a central part of yourself, difficult to start anew. Scary, too, because there are so many things uncertain about the new you—you have to learn what you want and how to react to things all over again. Is that what you're getting at?"

"Exactly! That's right. That's what I mean. Oh, I'm so glad you understand!"

"I'm surprised that anyone has any difficulty understanding you."

She fell silent for a moment as a memory invaded her mind. "I just remembered a dream I had a few days before I decided to take flying lessons, right before we met. I wanted to climb up to the roof of a tall building. I knew it would be dangerous, and I was afraid, but I knew I had to do it. I had to get to the roof of that building, or die trying, because not to make the top would be much worse than a fall to my death. As I climbed, people standing on the ground around the building yelled at me to come down, saying that I was stupid, that it was too dangerous. Then, when I finally made it and climbed out on the roof, the crowd became angry and started cursing and throwing rocks at me." She shivered. "I can hear them now. I felt envied and hated at the same time, Patten, but I knew I had to get there, whatever the cost. And I felt confident and free on that roof, in spite of all the rejection from the crowd and danger I had to endure to get there."

Suddenly feeling self-conscious, she smiled shyly. "I don't want to bore you," she said, "but the dream seemed to fit somehow. I'm surprised I remembered it."

"You never bore me, Carley." He looked at her intently. "You know, we both may have skipped the teenage years as we grew up; maybe we had too many serious things on our minds."

"I think you're right. And I think I've fallen in love with you," she said simply.

Patten was filled with warmth. "Too bad we don't have time for a motel room," he whispered.

"We'll have to make up for it later, my dear."

"Promise?"

"Oh, yes," she said, as she took a deep breath, swelling her chest.

Her timeless eyes, now turquoise, mesmerized him. Underneath the table, he pressed his leg against her. "I want you so badly," he whispered.

"Me too, but maybe we'd better take a walk," she spoke quietly, looking around to see whether anyone noticed them.

Patten rose unsteadily to his feet. "Of course you're right," he said.

Carley stood up. "Let's pay the bill before we leave this time," she winked.

They held hands and talked as they walked along the sidewalk and through the parking lots of the Doubletree and Red Line motels. At six o'clock, they took a taxi back to the airport and preflighted the King Air for the return trip. The businessmen returned, obviously pleased with their meeting, and they departed Austin for the quick return trip.

After hangaring the King Air at now-deserted Gulf Shores Aviation, Patten and Carley strolled to her car in the parking lot, Patten's arm around her small waist.

"You're so beautiful," he said as he held and kissed her. "And those businessmen thought so too," he added, with more than a hint of jealousy in his voice.

"Come on, Patten, how do you know?" she laughed.

"Well, they couldn't take their eyes off you. You saw them! You didn't hear what Jim Kimmel, the company manager, said to me when he was leaving?"

"Well, no, what did he say?" she asked.

"He said to 'bring that lovely woman along any time you want'!"

"He said that? Oh, he was just being nice," she protested.

"Ha! I saw them looking at you with their beady eyes! I'll tell you this, beautiful girl. I'm so jealous I could murder each one! But then again," he sighed pensively, "you *are* beautiful, and I can't blame them for looking."

"Oh! I am not!"

"And I will tell you something else, Carley," he said, seriously, "I enjoyed having you with me. I don't want to be without you, even for a short time. This is serious!"

"You're so sweet," she smiled. "I've never been so happy!"

He thought for a moment. "I used to like backpacking through the woods, Carley. I wonder if you'd go hiking with me, day hiking." He hadn't been backpacking since he lost Steve. "It's peaceful and quiet in the forest."

"I will go anywhere with you, darling, just to be with you. You should know that by now."

"Carley, listen, don't agree to go if you really don't want to. Some people don't like hiking in the woods. You sweat, you tire, and you fight insects. We can do something else if you don't like hiking."

"I want to go hiking with you, dear. I've never been hiking, but I know I'll love it. When and where?"

"Okay, but if we go and you don't like it, tell me and we'll turn back."

"All right, but don't worry. I'll love it!"

"There's a forest, a national forest, Bankhead, north of Birmingham. It's big. I've flown over the forest many times. We could fly to a nearby airport early one morning, get a courtesy vehicle to drive to the forest, then get back here by eight or nine in the evening. I would like to take Mark, but he's a little too young yet: his legs would give out. The trek is more than a stroll in the woods: it's about six miles in and six miles back if we go to the place I heard about."

"Sounds like fun. When do you want to go?"

"I'll get the forest ranger station there to send me some maps. Why don't we try to go next Thursday?"

"That's fine with me," she said.

He embraced and kissed her. "I know you have to get back to Mark, darling." He opened the car door for her.

"Yes, I have to be going. I wish I could stay."

Chapter Nineteen

After Linda left for the night, Patten picked up the telephone and punched in Carley's number.

"Oh, hi dear," Carley said as she recognized his voice. "I'm glad you called. We just finished dinner. Mark is playing in his room, and I'm sitting around missing you. Are you through for the day?"

"Yes, but I'm still at the airport. Everyone's gone. Why don't you come over for a few minutes? I want to see you, but I also want to show you something. Bring Mark, too," he added.

"A surprise? What is it? I love surprises!" she bubbled.

He loved her childlike enthusiasm. "It's something I'll have to show you. Come on over."

"We'll be there in a few minutes, dear."

Patten busied himself organizing his desk until the sound of tires on gravel signaled Carley and Mark's arrival. He unlocked the door to the parking lot, and met them at the door.

"Hello," he said to Carley, then turned to Mark who ran ahead into the office.

"Hi, Mark. I've a present for you!" He took Mark's hand and led him into the office. Opening the closet Patten pulled out a blue and white pedal airplane. He lifted Mark, who was wide-eyed with excitement, and put him in the cockpit.

Mark bubbled with excitement. "Mama, look! Can I have it, can I?"

"It's yours Mark. You can take it home with you when you go," Patten said.

"Mark, what do you say?" asked Carley.

Mark looked up. "Thank you!" He learned quickly to operate the pedals and steering wheel, but was hampered in his movements in the small office.

"Pedal it into the lobby, Mark. There's more room in there," Patten motioned for Mark to follow him as he walked down the hall into the lobby.

When Patten returned to Carley, he was pleased to see she was all smiles.

"What a thoughtful surprise," she said, as she touched his arm. "He's talked about nothing but airplanes since we went to Atlanta; he always wants to come to the airport and 'go fly with Mr. Forts'—he can't say 'Fortis' just yet. Thanks."

"His excitement is thanks enough, hon. But now let's look at the thing I wanted to show *you*."

While Mark played in the lobby, Patten led Carley into the classroom. He pointed to her shirttail now hanging with the others along the wall. On the shirttail Patten's artwork showed the Cessna one fifty-two flying downwind for runway one-eight. A figure on the ground was calling, "Come down! Come down!" The caption read: "Carley Price—solo flight—GREAT PILOT BUT CAN'T COUNT!"

"How's that?" he asked, chuckling. "You seem to have trouble counting touch-and-goes, as well as other, well, more important activities."

"Oh, you!" she said as she playfully hit him on the shoulder. "I can't help it if I'm excitable and get confused!"

"You excite me, always," he said as he tenderly held and kissed her.

"Oh, I'm so happy to be with you. I've had more happiness in the last few weeks than I've had in my whole life…and I thank you," she said as she looked up at him with moist eyes. "I hope you don't get tired of me saying that."

"You said the very words I was thinking," Patten said softly, as he held and kissed her. "It was my good karma that you came my way."

They were both suddenly aware of the change in sounds from the lobby. Mark's burbling and pedaling noises had stopped, and sounds of thrashing about filled the otherwise quiet offices.

"Mark? Mark?" Carley shouted.

Mark didn't answer. As they hurried into the lobby, they saw him writhing on the floor, and rushed to him. His face was flushed and he desperately clutched at his throat. Faint gurgling noises came from his open mouth. His eyes were wide with fear.

"I think he's choking on something!" Carley exclaimed as she held his mouth wide open and searched with her curled index finger. "But I can't feel anything!"

Patten raced into his office and returned with a flashlight and fingernail file.

"Hold his mouth open," Patten said. Carley did so, and Patten used the blunt end of the file to hold Mark's tongue down as he peered as best he could into the child's throat. With the flashlight, he could see pink flesh with red streaks of blood and a dark object too deep to reach and dislodge.

"He's swallowed something, Carley, something that's too deep in his throat for us to remove!"

Carley jerked Mark up and tried the Heimlich maneuver, but without success. She then bent him over her left arm and struck him in the back with her right hand. The object would not eject.

Mark's condition quickly deteriorated: his face and hands turned blue, his eyes rolled back in his head with the white only visible, and he struggled weakly.

"It won't come out! We'll have to get him to the emergency room!" Carley was shouting now.

Patten put his hand on her shoulder. "Wait! That's at least fifteen minutes from here."

"Should we call 911 for the rescue squad?"

"That would take too long!"

"He's choking to death! What can we do!?" Carley was shouting.

"Just a minute!" Patten knew what had to be done. He felt defeated. Sweat popped out on his forehead as he ran to the flight instruction room and brought back a box of razor blades and bottle of alcohol from a cabinet. Taking one blade out, he held it in one hand and poured alcohol over it with the other.

"Put Mark on the couch," he said tightly.

"What are you going to do?" Carley questioned, close to tears as she placed Mark's now unconscious and limp body that had turned a sickly bluish black color, on the couch.

Perspiration ran down Patten's face. He felt as though an outside force was compelling him towards his execution. "Carley, Mark has to have some oxygen," he said in as calm a voice as he could muster. "I'm going to perform a tracheotomy. It's a simple procedure, but there'll be some blood. We'll open an airway below the obstruction."

Patten looked quickly around the room until his eyes fixed on a large plastic straw in Mark's soft drink cup. He grabbed it and bathed it in alcohol.

She looked at him in disbelief: "Do you…do you…?"

"Don't worry. I can do this, but I need your help. Hold his chin back."

Patten used the razor to cut a small opening through the soft tissue and cartilage of the trachea below the laryngeal prominence. Blood formed around and oozed out of the incision. Patten rolled Mark over on his side, swiftly cut off and threw away half the plastic straw, and pushed the other half gently but firmly through the opening. He blew on the straw and blood bubbled around it. Rolling Mark over on his back again, he pushed gently but firmly on Mark's chest. Respiration was weak at first, but became stronger as the life-giving oxygen dispersed through Mark's body.

"Will he be alright? Will he live?" Carley asked, close to panic.

"Yes, he's breathing. His color is returning and he's regaining consciousness. But we'll have to take him to the ER now so that the obstruction can be removed and the incision closed."

Blood flowed freely. While Carley determinedly held Mark's hands, Patten took a handful of freshly laundered cleaning cloths from a closet and wrapped them low on the child's neck. He locked Mark's arms against his chest and carried him through the doorway while Carley held the door to the parking lot open.

"Will you drive, please?" she asked.

"Sure. Hold him on his side and don't let him push or pull on the straw."

Once she was seated on the passenger side of the front seat, Patten handed Mark to her. He squirmed more strongly now, but Carley held him by anchoring his legs with hers, squeezing his arms against her with her left arm, and tilting his head back with her right hand. The cleaning cloths spread underneath Mark's neck were quickly soaked with blood, as was Mark's shirt. He tried to cry, but only muffled and gurgling sounds came from him.

Patten spoke softly into Mark's ear: "Mark you're going to be okay, but be as quiet and still as you can for a few minutes."

"Carley, can you manage him?"

"I think so! Let's go!"

"Hold his head down a little so that blood will not flow down his throat."

Patten raced toward the hospital with hazard lights flashing, while Carley at times had to use all her strength to keep Mark still. She tried to calm him by telling him, over and over, that he was going to be all right.

"Back there," she said to Patten, "where did you learn how to do that?"

Patten hesitated and took a deep breath. "It's a long story. I'll tell you sometime. But I need for you to keep this between us. I don't have a license to practice medicine."

"Well...sure, but I do want you to tell me later what this is all about..." She tightened her grip on Mark as he renewed his squirming.

"Of course," he said resignedly.

"Is something wrong?" she asked.

"It's personal," he replied, as he turned into the emergency entrance at the hospital. He parked in front of the emergency room doors. "Why don't I take Mark?" he asked, as he opened her door.

"Thanks."

They rushed into the emergency room lobby, which was almost empty. "This child needs attention quickly. Where's the physician?" Patten asked of the seated receptionist, who had glanced up from paperwork as they entered.

The receptionist, a middle-aged blonde wearing bifocal eyeglasses over a pointed nose, reached for some forms from a tray atop her desk. "He's taking a break now. But you'll need to talk to me first, sir."

Patten, carrying Mark, walked past her and kicked open the double doors that led back to the treatment rooms. Carley followed close behind.

"Sir, you can't go in there!" the receptionist called as she left her desk to catch him.

"Doctor! Doctor!" Patten shouted down the hallway.

A physician and nurse appeared from one of the cubicles. The physician handed his cup of coffee to the nurse. Patten carried Mark to him, and glanced at the nameplate on the white coat.

"Dr. Witt, this child has something lodged in his throat. He's breathing through…"

The receptionist interrupted him: "Doctor, this man barged in here without…"

"Okay, Ms. Johnson, we'll take care of that later," the physician said to the receptionist, who whirled about quickly and stomped away muttering something about hospital rules and regulations. Then he eyed Mark, "I see. He's able to breath through this piece of plastic straw. Bring him in and put him on the table," he said as he entered a treatment cubicle. "Nurse, call Dr. Thomas!"

A second nurse appeared, and Dr. Witt instructed her to restrain Mark on the table. Patten removed the blood-soaked cloths from his shoulder and threw them into a wastebasket. He took Carley by the arm and led her into the hallway.

"If you don't need me here anymore, I think I'd better be going. Mark's in good hands now. He's going to be okay."

"Yes, of course. I'll call my mother-in-law if I need any help. You can't know how much I thank you," she added.

"Glad to be of help, Carley. Call me when you can, whatever the time. I'll park your car in the lot and leave the keys with the receptionist. I can get a taxi home. Don't forget to call me!"

He went to the restroom, washed his hands and toweled off his face. The memory of the first and last time he was here passed through his mind: it seemed an eternity ago, but he could still hear the hollow ringing sound of the flushing toilet.

Returning to the lobby, he approached the front desk. The receptionist looked at him sullenly.

"Ms. Johnson, the child needed immediate medical attention, and I didn't see any real medical emergencies here in the lobby when I came in. I do appreciate what a difficult job you have and apologize for being inconsiderate." *She's detached and compulsive, the only way to survive in her job.*

Her face softened a little. "It's just that we have these rules to go by, and I have these forms to fill in, you know," she said as she shuffled through the pages.

"Yes, I understand. The lady with the child is Carley Price. As soon as Dr. Witt and the child can do without her, she'll come out to the desk and give you any information you need. I'm going to park her car out of the way, and then leave the keys with you. Will that do?"

"Well, yes, I guess so," she said, still obviously miffed. "Then you're not the father? You can't give me the information?"

"No," Patten replied, then turned and left the lobby. He drove the short distance to the airport and put Mark's airplane in the trunk. Driving back to the hospital, he parked the car and returned Carley's keys to the receptionist.

* * *

Patten grabbed the phone at the first ring.

"Hi dear. I hated to bother you at this time of night. Do you know it's almost four in the morning?"

"No bother, I've been waiting for your call. How's Mark?"

Carley sounded tired but peaceful. "I'm still at the hospital. Mark's fine. The doctors here were able to dislodge a small building block from his throat, and to sew up the opening you made that saved his life. They gave him a sedative, and he's sleeping peacefully. I guess he brought the block in his pocket to your office. He's just being kept here for observation for a few hours…he'll be discharged at eleven this morning."

"Great. And how're you doing, hon. I know you must be exhausted."

"I'm okay, just a little tired."

"I felt I was letting you and Mark down, leaving you at the hospital…"

Carley broke in: "Don't you dare say that! You saved his life! All I did was sit around here worrying, not able to do anything helpful."

"Sometimes sitting around worrying is the hardest part. I was impressed with the way you jumped in to help Mark, though. I've been sitting here thinking what you've gone through, trying to take care of Mark by yourself. Jack hasn't been around to help in those hundred emergencies you've probably had with this child. You're a strong woman, Carley. I admire you."

"Well, thanks Patten. But I wasn't successful. If you hadn't been there—well, I can't bear to think what would've happened," she said in a shaky voice. "I can't imagine where you learned to do that. You're the one to be admired!"

"Carley, you jumped in and did what you knew to do. A hundred other times what you did would have worked—happened not to work this time. But you did what you could, and very well, and that's what counts!"

"Thanks, darling. But what you did with Mark, the, uh, tracheotomy? I know you don't have to learn that to be a flight instructor," she laughed uncertainly. "Will you tell me sometimes?"

He stiffened. "Yes, babe."

"You don't sound happy about it."

"I'll tell you later."

"All right, I can wait."

"I will tell you."

After a short silence, Patten said, "Carley?"

"Yes, dear?"

"The receptionist wanted to know if I were the father. I wish I were."

"Oh, I wish you were, too," she said in a broken voice.

"I put Mark's airplane in the trunk of your car. Talk to you tomorrow night?"

"Please."

"Let me know if you need anything."

Chapter Twenty

A few days later in the early dawn Patten and Carley departed Gulf Shores Aviation for Posey Airport near Haleyville, a small town at the edge of Bankhead National Forest. The sky was overcast with thick stratus. When Patten called the flight service station and filed for five thousand feet on an instrument flight plan, he received a weather report that called for patchy fog at Posey to burn off prior to their estimated time of arrival, and for clear conditions to prevail throughout the day and evening.

Carley, in the left seat for practice at piloting while relying solely on instruments, aimed the Cherokee one-forty, a bit less robust than the Cherokee one-eighty, north into the stratus. All outside visual references vanished as the airplane cut into the dark mist. Carley's hands tightened on the yoke as she began to scan the flight instruments.

"Climb at eighty five knots, babe, and relax. We'll shortly be on top!"

"I don't know if I'll ever get used to this! It's unnerving when you can't see where you're going," Carley said. She glanced over at Patten, who looked relaxed and happy. His confidence was contagious, and she gradually allowed herself to relax her grip on the yoke and sink into the seat.

A TIME IN THE SUN

The Cherokee soon broke through the ragged top of the stratus layer out into the bright sunshine at 4,300 feet.

"Yeeee Hawwww!" Patten yelled. In his mind he heard the prelude to Tchaikovsky's piano concerto number one. "Do you hear that?"

"What?"

"Music! I heard music when you broke out of the clouds," he grinned playfully at her.

She turned and looked at him oddly. "What's happened to you? I haven't seen you like this before. Are you going crazy on me, guy?"

Patten laughed. "I've been crazy; now I'm going sane!"

Her eyes sparkled. "You know something, my love? You're weird!" She surveyed the rolling carpet of white clouds beneath them. "It's always breathtaking above the clouds!" she exclaimed.

Patten called the flight service station, as he had been asked to do when he filed the flight plan, and reported the altitude of the cloud tops. The clouds below them disappeared as they flew north. Nearing Haleyville, Patten pointed out the vast forests, rivers, and lakes below that formed the Bankhead Forest.

The single runway at Posey Airport soon appeared in the distance. The fog had lifted as predicted. Patten called the Anniston Flight Service Station and canceled the IFR flight plan. Carley throttled back, descended, and landed smoothly on the single runway.

"That was a greaser, beautiful woman! Excellent landing!"

"Was it? Do you really think I'll make a pilot?" Carley was ecstatic.

"Undoubtedly!"

A lineman stood out on the ramp in front of the small FBO, and used standard hand signals to direct them to a tie down spot.

Leaving instructions to top off the one-forty, Patten and Carley took the courtesy vehicle, a pick-up truck that the FBO was generous to loan to them. The couple crawled into the vehicle and removed a sunscreen from the windshield.

Patten read to Carley the warning stamped on the sunscreen: "REMOVE FROM WINDSHIELD BEFORE DRIVING." He chuckled, "Wouldn't you hope that anyone able to drive would have enough judgment to remove the screen before driving off? What is this, babe? A statement on the level of intelligence of current American drivers? Or perhaps it's only recognition of the current litigious atmosphere of the country."

Carley laughed. "I don't know. The instructions may be necessary. Baseball caps don't come with instructions, and look at the way some guys wear them. Maybe some would try and drive on instruments!"

"Yes, that's true!"

Patten folded the sunscreen and started driving the short distance toward Bankhead forest. He stopped at a convenience store to pick up snacks and sandwiches, and stuffed them into the Kelty backpack he had brought along. Patten filled with water two canteens he had kept from his backpacking days.

After studying the map, they drove out Highway 195, turned left on 93, then right on 60, traveling east on the narrow and rough but asphalted road past the Sipsey Wilderness picnic area. Turning left on a gravel road, they drove to a small bridge, now blocked to vehicles, which crossed the narrow and shallow Borden creek.

Looking over a trail map, completing a form and depositing the required dollar in a box provided nearby, Patten then slipped on the backpack, and he and Carley traversed the bridge and climbed up a long hill to begin the hike. The first part of the trail appeared to be an old logging road, grown up with weeds and partially blocked in several places by downed trees, mostly pines, that had been ravaged by pine beetles.

Occasionally they had to climb over or around tree trunks. The trail then wound along a ridge with mixed pine and hardwood trees at either side. Hemlock, sycamore, oak, cherry, and large-leafed deciduous magnolias formed canopies on both sides. This part of the trail was often wide enough for them to walk side by side. They held hands and kept up a steady, carefree conversation.

Carley often remarked how pretty and serene the woods looked. Patten was pleased that she liked the forest, which had been a favorite place of his since childhood.

They passed a patch of green pasture, a food plot that was carved out of the woods to feed the whitetail deer during the winter. Several side trails led off to the left. Patten and Carley consulted the map repeatedly in an attempt to find trail 204.

At length they turned off on a trail to the left, and although there was no trail marker in sight they felt they had gone far enough to intercept trail 204. They wound down the narrow path, often passing large hardwoods that had been uprooted by an ice storm the past winter, and tornadic winds in the spring. The leaves were still green on some of the trees, suggesting that storm damage had occurred only recently.

Eventually the trail became more of a downgrade. After walking several minutes they came to a fork in the trail. A trail marker, pointing left for trail 204, convinced them they had been on the correct trail. Now they took the right fork, following the directions on the trail map to the Big Tree, which was marked prominently with an "X" on the small map. They hiked down a slope that first curved to the right and then to the left. Large boulders appeared along the trail. Almost immediately a dull roar sounded in the distance. The path became very steep, so that in some places it was necessary to hold onto small saplings to maintain balance.

The noise grew louder as they picked their way down into a deep gorge that had been carved out by water eons ago. At the floor of the gorge they both looked around in awe at the surreal scene. Large boulders were strewn about. To the right, at the upper end of the gorge, the source of the sound was evident: water cascaded down a cliff onto smooth rock below. Water from the waterfall formed a small creek that rushed down the gorge to the Sipsey River, a mile or two down the gorge.

Some thirty yards down from the waterfall was the largest poplar tree that either Patten or Carley had ever seen. Names and dates, some very old, were carved on the tree. Neither Patten nor Carley wanted to risk damaging the tree by carving on it, but they left their initials on a large boulder nearby.

"When I called the ranger station I was told that this poplar tree is the oldest tree in Alabama, estimated to be more than five hundred years old. I guess it's lasted this long because down here it's protected from storms. Can you imagine that this tree was probably here when Columbus landed?" Patten asked.

"It's awesome to consider," Carley agreed.

"Finally, I found something older than me," Patten smiled.

"Oh, come on!"

They sat and rested beside the small creek created by the waterfall. The air was crisp, clean and cool.

The sides of the gorge were steep bluffs, some impassable without climbing gear. The bluffs were overhanging at several places, creating caves beneath. The caves around the waterfall invited interest, and they spent more than an hour picking their way around boulders to explore the caves.

Returning to an open spot downstream from the large poplar tree, they unloaded snacks from the pack. Patten leaned the backpack against a rock, and sat resting his back on the pack. Carley sat facing him on the forest floor as they ate lunch.

Carley then leaned her back against him with her head nestled on his chest. He cradled her in his arms, his lips nuzzling her neck and ears. The cacophony of sounds of the forest and the waterfall was serene yet somehow invigorating.

"It's so peaceful here, and I'm so happy to be with you." She lazily reached back and stroked the side of his face.

"I'm glad Mark was doing well and you could come with me."

"His grandmother was eager to keep him, so things worked out. He's running around as though nothing ever happened to him. He doesn't know how close he was to death. You saved his life, dear. I'll never be able to thank you enough!"

"I'm just glad I could help. By the way, what did the physician say about the emergency incision I made?"

"He asked me who had performed the operation." She suddenly wheeled around to face Patten, the memory bringing fire to her eyes. "He had the gall to warn me that a blood vessel might have been severed and Mark could have bled to death! I asked him if Mark, unable to breathe, would have survived fifteen or twenty minutes to reach the emergency room since he was already unconscious and blue before he could even have been put in the car. He said probably not, and backed off. Nothing else was said. Humph! I get angry all over again just thinking about it!"

Patten smiled. "I see that you do, hon. And that warms me, for some reason."

She relaxed, turned and resumed her position against him.

He squeezed her back against his chest. "Carley?"

"Yes, dear."

"I wanted you to come with me today not only so I could enjoy this place with you and to be with you all day, but I want to tell you something: I love you, Carley."

She sat up and turned toward him, her face soft. "Oh, you don't know how I've wanted to hear you say those words, dear. I've loved you for a long time, but I didn't know if you loved me. I knew you cared for me, but I wanted you to love me as I love you."

"It's difficult for me to say that word. I don't know exactly why. It's an important word; I can't use it lightly, my love. I've loved you for some time. You know that I tried to keep my distance from you, but couldn't. Now I'm glad I couldn't. I don't want you out of my sight."

He went on: "Darling, I don't make much money, much profit, from the flight school back at Gulf Shores. I get by. I eat. I pay my rent. I make the airplane payments. The business is growing. But," he added with a touch of resignation, "wealth and piloting separated after Charles Lindberg and Howard Hughes, I'm afraid. The two words don't mix together very well these days, except maybe for airline pilots. Most pilots fly mainly for reasons other than money."

"But why are you talking about finances?" she said quizzically.

"I love you. I don't want to do without you, hon. I hate to go on and on about this, but I want to be with you all the time."

"What are you saying? Do you want me to marry you, dear?"

"Well, yes," he awkwardly answered, "but…"

She interrupted him. "Oh darling, of course I'll marry you!" she said as she grabbed and kissed him.

He laughed. "Well, that's great, hon! But there *are* a couple of little problems here."

"What?" she said, guardedly.

"Well, for one thing, you're already married," he laughed again. "A little technicality—did you forget?"

She laughed. "Almost. I don't really have a marriage though, dear. Jack doesn't write or call. He doesn't really need a marriage! I love you, Patten, and want to be with you forever. I don't care about the money."

"Jack must make good money, and I wanted you to realize what you would be giving up."

"He's paid well. But I was so unhappy before I met you. A choice between you broke and Jack with money is no contest."

"And I am older than you. What if we were just married, and I suddenly fell over with a heart attack?"

She thought for a moment. "Darling, if we had two months together, I know they'd be wonderful months! Two wonderful months is better than none at all. Anyway, silly, I could have a heart attack and die before you!"

"I just want to be sure you know what you'd be getting into."

"Well, what about you? What about Mark?"

He thought about Mark, and about Steve. He remembered Steve at Mark's age. A memory flashed in his mind: he came home, tired from the office, and Steve ran out to meet him at the door. He picked Steve up, high in the air, then clutched him to his chest, and filled his face with kisses. Steve, in turn, covered Patten with wet kisses, all the while gurgling happily. He saw Steve, as an infant, sleeping on his chest, wrestling around on the floor as a toddler, shopping together, going to Disney World, enjoying rides at the fair, helping him with homework, and teaching him the computer.

He kissed her tenderly. "I want the whole package. I need Mark, too."

"You do? Oh, he would be happy to have you as his father."

She again leaned her back against him, relaxing in his arms. "If this isn't heaven, it's close."

They relaxed contentedly for a long time. Carley eventually broke the silence, asking lazily, "Patten, how did you get involved in flying and flight instruction?"

"Oh, I don't know. I suppose my interest in flying goes back to childhood. My father was a pilot in the military—that probably has something to do with it, I've learned. As a young boy I used to build model airplanes with glue and balsam wood." He chuckled, "I never knew that kids sniffed the glue for a high, until I was much older. I used it to glue the little pieces of wood together.

"I've been a pilot only about four years, though, love. I first flew crop dusters, but tired of that, and did some flight instruction and banner towing in Panama City. Then I had the occasion to land at the Gulf Shores Airport several months ago. I liked it. The owner of the FBO, Leland Robertson, was having trouble making ends meet. He doesn't like paperwork, so I made a deal with him to furnish me space for flight instruction for one year, for free, and I would do the paperwork for him to bid on a contract to refuel military and civilian government aircraft at the airport. In addition, I would buy fuel from him and rent hangar space for flight instruction and towing of advertising banners. He was awarded the government contract, and with the extra income he's happy with the way things have worked out."

Carley sat up, and turned to look at Patten. "Looks like you have a busy airport, dear, and you're filled up with students."

"We're growing, love."

He held Carley close. "I don't want to go, but we'd better be starting back if we want to make Gulf Shores by nine o'clock," he said. "It's six miles back to the truck, you know."

"I didn't know I could walk that far. But, I don't want to leave, dear, and I don't want you to turn me loose," she said, contentedly.

"We should have brought our sleeping bags."

"Can we sleep in the same bag?" she wondered.

"We can zip two bags together."

"Then let's do that the next time," she pleaded.

"Let's do," he murmured as he kissed her again. "It'll be good getting into backpacking again if you find you like it."

Shortly afterwards they climbed out of the gorge and hiked back to the truck. After paying for the fuel and thanking the helpful and friendly lineman at Posey, they flew back to Gulf Shores and were on the ground by 8:30 p.m.

* * *

A few days later Patten awoke early in the morning with a severe headache and fever. He felt nauseated and ached all over. His wrists and knees were painful, especially with motion, and a rash broke out on his right arm. He couldn't think clearly or concentrate well, and became dizzy when he made abrupt moves.

He telephoned Carley but received no answer. He then called Linda to cancel his appointments for the day, explaining to her that he didn't feel well. He waited around the duplex until nine o'clock, then found a physician's office in the telephone directory, called and was told he could be seen that morning. Physicians in the area were used to receiving call-ins from tourists, which was a large part of their business in the area. Patten didn't have a regular physician, as he usually didn't need one, although he did go for a flight physical regularly to an FAA approved physician in Mobile.

The physician, a middle-aged balding man with a closely cropped beard, listened with interest to Patten's description of his symptoms after taking blood pressure and temperature. Patten's blood pressure was up and his temperature was 102 degrees.

"You've probably come down with one of the strains of flu virus going around Mr. Fortis," he said.

Patten chose his words carefully, but felt so badly that he found it difficult to be tactful. "A friend had these same symptoms once, and was diagnosed as having Lyme disease, I think it's called. He got it from a tick bite. I was in the woods a few days ago and afterwards found a tick embedded in my right arm when I took a shower."

"Lyme disease is fairly rare around here." The physician scratched his chin. "Excuse me a moment," he said as he stepped out of the examination room.

"This guy was given a prescription for an antibiotic, tetracycline as I recall—cleared him up," Patten called after him. He held his head in his hands: talking loudly made his head pound.

The physician returned in a few moments with an open medical journal, and examined the rash on Patten's arm. "You do have symptoms of Lyme disease, Mr. Fortis. Don't see much of that around here," he said.

"I was in Bankhead Forest a few days ago."

"Your blood pressure is up, too, 160/90. Does your blood pressure run high?"

"No, it doesn't." Patten rubbed his forehead and his neck to relieve the pain. The movement of his wrists was painful, and he winced.

"You're in pretty much pain, though, huh?"

"Yes, I am."

"The pain has undoubtedly made your pressure high. Pain makes the pressure go up, you know."

"Yes. I guess that's it," Patten agreed.

The physician found a prescription pad among papers on a shelf and scribbled on two sheets, handing them to Patten. "I've written prescriptions for an antibiotic and pain killer to take as needed. Take the entire antibiotic, even if you begin to feel well in a couple of days. If you get worse, or don't improve, come back to see me."

Patten stopped on his way home and had the prescriptions filled for the analgesic and antibiotic medication. After taking the antibiotic, he pulled off his clothes and crawled into bed. He telephoned Carley but still received no answer. He took the phone off the hook and tried to read, but couldn't concentrate because of the pain, so he put the book away and slid a Yanni CD in the player. With the volume low he settled back in bed to try to sleep. He felt miserable.

He was drawn from predormition by the ringing of his doorbell. He tried to ignore it, but the ringing was as persistent as his headache, so he grudgingly arose and slipped on a housecoat, determined to use all the energy he could muster to kill any solicitor he found at the door. When he opened the door, he was shocked to see Carley.

"Hello, dear." she said lightly and smiled, but her apprehensive eyes betrayed her true feelings as she examined his face.

"What are you doing here?" He was glad to see her, but worried that she might be seen.

"Well, that's some greeting to give a person you said you loved, dear! Aren't you going to invite me in?"

"Of course! Come on in. I'm just so surprised to see you," he pulled her inside and closed the door. "You may have problems if you're seen!"

She hugged him. "I was worried about you. Linda said you called in sick and canceled your appointments. I've been out shopping early this morning. I tried to call you, but first got no answer and then only a busy signal."

"I tried you a couple of times, too, hon."

She felt his forehead. "You have a fever, and you look like you must feel terrible. Are you in pain somewhere?"

He sighed. "A little headache and pains here and there," he shrugged. "I've been to a physician this morning and started a prescription. I may have Lyme disease from a tick bite. Did you find any ticks on you after we returned from Bankhead?"

She shook her head. "No, I'm fine. Never been healthier." She eyed him suspiciously. "You have more than 'a little headache and pains here and there,'" she mocked him. "Is the Lyme disease serious?"

He smiled, embarrassed, at her concern. "If you catch it early and take an antibiotic you're usually cured. Delayed diagnosis or misdiagnosis can complicate matters, though, I understand."

"I know you feel terrible, dear. I've got plenty of time, and I'm staying here with you to help out."

In spite of his pain, Patten felt self-conscious. "No, thanks Carley, I'll be fine with a little rest and this antibiotic," he protested.

Carley was hurt. "I love you, darling. I see you're sick and want to help! You've done so much for me. Why won't you let me help you? Why won't you let yourself need me? You do everything for me and Mark and will let me do nothing for you! Do you understand what I mean? I want this to be a two-way street!"

He recoiled from the intensity of her feeling, and then pulled her to him, as he was overcome with warmth and love for her.

"Why don't you lie down, dear," she said as she guided him to bed.

He put up little resistance. He lay down, and Carley fluffed a pillow to put under his head. He dropped off into a hot and restless sleep, then quickly awoke thrashing around in bed and struggling to scream, but couldn't make a sound. Carley was at his side trying to comfort him. He lay breathing heavily until he recovered from the nightmare enough to get himself up. He sat on the side of the bed and pushed the palms of his hands into his eyes.

"What's wrong, dear? Are you okay? I think you were having a bad dream."

He had difficulty organizing his thoughts. He stood, and held onto Carley beside the bed. "Yes, a nightmare. Oh Carley, I don't want to hurt you. You mean everything to me. I do need you. I'm just not used to anyone helping me, I guess. I'm afraid I'd burden and overwhelm you. My mother always became hysterical when I was sick or injured." He wept as he held her close.

He was suddenly dizzy and staggered. Carley took his arm and sat him back on the bed. He was in no condition to argue while the room was spinning. To keep from falling he kneeled down, leaning over on the bed. Carley sat on the bed and rested his head in her lap.

He felt miserable. "My mother always complained about her health. She wanted me to stay close to home, to take care of her when she was ill—I brought things for her, medicines, glasses of water, and the like. I did what I could but she was never better."

"What about your father, why didn't he take care of her?" Carley asked.

Patten sighed, "Mother and father were never close. He was in the military, a pilot I think I told you, and was gone most of the time, and when he *was* home they argued continuously. They eventually divorced. I suppose mother depended on my sister and me—mostly me—for some reason."

Carley fell silent for a moment. "Your mother asked you for help, you tried, but she never felt better. I guess you wanted to leave home as soon as you were old enough to get out."

"Well, sure, I did, but I felt guilty, as though I should stay and take care of the family, hon, although I obviously wasn't helping her." He looked at her and smiled, in spite of the discomfort. "We were one of those 'dysfunctional families' you hear about these days."

"Lot of them around, dear. Mine, too. What did you do, then, sweet?

I'm dying to know more about you, and I often feel you don't want to tell me very much."

He rubbed his head. "I didn't think much about a career, Carley, but I allowed myself to be talked, by my mother, into applying for medical school, and was accepted. It just lately occurred to me that she wanted me to be a physician to better help her! Anyway, I guess since that pleased her, I didn't feel so much that I was abandoning the family. I went to medical school, never liked it, but stuck with it anyway, married and worked in a clinic for several years. Then—"

Carley interrupted: "Oh, that's where you learned what to do to help Mark…"

"In general, yes," he agreed. "I studied and interned at a hospital where tracheotomies were performed. But," he confessed, "I'd never performed one alone. I assisted in the ER. In my practice I'd never had to do one; most physicians haven't unless they've worked in trauma centers or ER's. Can you believe that? But I thought I could," he went on, "and Mark needed to breathe. I'm glad that it turned out well—I don't think I could have lived with myself if it hadn't."

Carley broke a short silence. "You left your medical practice to pilot airplanes?"

"Yes. I never felt that I fitted in the medical profession: it was not what I wanted to do. I can't tell you the reason I first chose medicine as a career, except that mother was pushing me."

Painfully he looked up at Carley, the fever reducing his defenses. "And, there were some other reasons I changed careers. I'm so ashamed to tell you this, Carley, but I had a child patient, Johnny Simmons, to die while he was in my care. He was in the hospital, in pain from a broken arm, and over the telephone I gave an order for morphine. The nurse gave him an adult dose, and he died! I was so upset I could barely function. Then, a couple of weeks later my only child, Steve, died of an overdose of a street drug one of the kids at a party slipped into his punch."

"Oh, no!"

He sobbed. "Forgive me for being so emotional, but I felt responsible for both deaths. Steve was only 14, and Johnny was just 7 years old. They were in my care, and I let them down.

"I was agonizing over the patient's death when Steve died, and I suppose I became something of a zombie afterwards. There was a malpractice suit filed against the nurse, the hospital and me. Since I had given the order over the phone, it was the nurse's word against mine. When the time came to give a deposition I was so depressed I could hardly function. I didn't really care how the lawsuit turned out—didn't care one way or the other. I suppose the defense attorneys for the malpractice carrier saw what an inept witness I'd be so they opted to settle out of court."

Carley hugged him. "My God, you went through a terrible time! I don't see how you survived. I wish I'd been with you. I know what a tragedy it must have been to lose that child, your patient, and a little later your only son," she said strongly, "but it wasn't your fault! It wasn't your fault for either death, dear. I don't know much about medical practices, but I bet all doctors who've been in practice for a long time have lost a patient by accident, misunderstanding, or something else."

"Well, I've heard that medical treatment is the third leading cause of death," he said sarcastically. "But, thank you for saying that, Carley. I suppose it's true. I always felt, though, that the child was entrusted to me because he was a patient of mine, and that Steve was dependent on me and looked to me for protection, because I was his father, and I failed my obligations."

"Anyone who knows you will know that you take your obligations very seriously. I'd put my life, or Mark's, in your hands anytime, in medicine, or in flying," she smiled.

"I now know that you would, hon. I apologize for keeping this from you, Carley. It just hurt so much that I didn't want to think about it for years. I just tried to survive. When Steve or Johnny came into my mind, I would hurt down to my soul. I couldn't live like that. I just tried to push the pain out of my head, and to keep to myself so that I wouldn't hurt anyone anymore, and wouldn't have to suffer that guilt."

He was pensive for a moment. "Janice was depressed, too, and blamed me for her embarrassment in the community, with the publicity and lawsuit. I was too depressed to give her emotional support. As I told you before, Carley, she filed for divorce, and I signed the papers her attorney drew up. I gave her everything except enough money to pay for flight training. I just felt unable to cope with taking care of anyone else and left medicine altogether."

"I can understand why, dear." Tears slowly trickled down Carley's cheeks. "You told me a little about this before, and I wondered why you never thought you were entitled to some support from Janice. I guess I understand, now…now that you've told me about your mom. I'm beginning to understand more about you, dear. Thanks for trusting me."

He told her of his constant attempts, after the tragedy and divorce, to isolate himself from others. He sobbed when he explained to her that the isolation worked for a time, but then he began coming apart mentally, discovered that he was very lonely, and how knowing her had helped to rescue him.

His head was pounding. He arose to get pain medication, but Carley took his arm and sat him back down. She gave him the medication and a glass of water, and then sat beside him on the bed.

"Old habits are tough to break," Patten grinned, despite his pain.

"I'll help you break those habits, I promise. I think I'm beginning to understand you more," she said as she dabbed at her eyes with a tissue. "I'm so happy you finally let me in on you. I loved you before, but if possible, more so now. I guess understanding makes love grow."

"I must warn you though," she asserted after a short pause, "I'm going to take care of you, so you're going to have to get used to it. *I can handle it! I won't fall apart.*" She kissed his forehead and ran her fingers through his hair.

"I don't think you will, judging from what I've seen in you. Mark sees you as a strong person who'll protect him."

"When you were a kid you had no one you could depend on to take care of you. Your mother leaned on you, and your father was gone."

Patten felt emotionally drained. The Lorcet Plus was beginning to work and his pain lessened. He felt silly and sheepishly smiled at her at first as she was fussing over him, but then he let himself go and began to enjoy the attention and care.

"This is great!" he said. "With this kind of treatment I may turn into a hypochondriac, or act like one!"

"I'm so glad that you like it—makes me feel important and satisfies some of my needs," she said softly.

He yawned contentedly. "I've cried more in the past four months than I have in the last forty years. After Johnny's and Steve's death I wanted to cry, but couldn't."

"It's time you cried. You've had good reason to cry, dear. Now, I'll bet you felt so badly you didn't get any sleep last night. I'm going to see if I can find some soup in the kitchen to heat up for you. Why don't you go to bed and rest now? Maybe you'll sleep better this time. I'll awaken you when it's ready."

He looked around the apartment. "The place is a mess; I haven't been a good housekeeper lately."

"Don't worry about it and crawl into bed," she demanded.

Carley left for the kitchen while Patten pulled his housecoat off and crawled under the covers. The last thing he remembered before he dozed off was thinking how great it was to have Carley there.

He was dreaming, in his feverish sleep, of Carley nestled up to him in bed, with her warm and silken body pressed tightly against his. He moaned with pleasure, taking her into his arms, and holding her close. He was passionately aware of her warmth, her smooth skin against him with all the bulges and depressions in the right places. His dream sleep slowly faded as he became aware of Carley's body against his.

"Wha...," he started to say, but his words were smothered by her kiss. Her lips were soft, hot and swollen against his lips, cheeks, neck, and eyelids. A mixture of passion and fever made him burning hot all over.

She crawled on top of him and climaxed several times before he allowed himself to reach peak excitement, holding off as long as he could to prolong the ecstasy. She eventually rolled over, but continued kissing him passionately.

"Darling, I hope you'll excuse me," she said breathlessly. "I think I'm so weird sometimes. I know you're sick, but I was overcome with desire. I don't know why...you excite me anyway, but there was something about...about taking care of you...you're being sick and feverish...and us being so in love...Oh, I don't know...I don't know! I only know that I just had to have you now and wanted to give myself to you!"

Patten chuckled. "You do that anytime you want, hon. Let's just call that a part of the treatment!"

Chapter Twenty-One

They put in three rigorous hours of flight training, covering all of the flight maneuvers that Carley would be tested on by an FAA examiner in Montgomery. They then spent two hours in the classroom on the oral test she would be given by the examiner, and on the navigation planning she would have to do.

"You'll have no problem on the exam, Carley. Your flying is great and your score was 92 on the written test. You'll have no trouble on the oral," he said confidently.

"I'll have one problem," she whispered. "I'll be missing you."

"Not for long, if I have anything to do with it," he whispered back to her. "Will you call me when you get back tomorrow, if I'm not here?"

"Yes. But what if I fail the test? You'll be disappointed in me, won't you?"

"You won't fail the test, Carley, but if you do, we'll go back over everything and re-take the test. And, no, I would not be disappointed in you, but I would be unhappy with myself: I would think I failed as your instructor. But you've learned well and you're more skillful than most 100-hour pilots—you'll barely have the required 40 hours of flight training when you take your test!

"One suggestion, though. Most of us can't go through all of the maneuvers without making at least one mistake. If you're told to perform a maneuver, and it doesn't turn out perfectly well, tell the examiner the mistake you made, then forget it! Go on to the next maneuver; think only of the next maneuver. Don't let the one mistake dominate your mind or spoil the flight."

"I understand, dear, but with you as my instructor, how could I fail?"

He chuckled. "And with you as my student, how could I fail?"

* * *

He was at the airport early Saturday morning to help Carley fill out her application for the private pilot license examination, and to sign her off for the cross-country trip to Montgomery as well as the examination itself. The weather was clear and forecast to be clear with ten miles visibility throughout the day, and only scattered cumulus clouds in the afternoon. Carley departed Gulf Shores looking more confident than most students.

Patten spent the morning pulling banners up and down the coast, and the afternoon training students. He was with a student practicing stalls and flight at minimum controllable airspeed when he heard Carley call in for an airport advisory.

After Linda gave the wind and traffic, Patten keyed the mike: "Eight Delta Tango, Zero Eight Quebec, is there a new private pilot at the controls? Over."

Carley's bubbly voice came through the headset, "Eight Delta Tango—that's affirmative!"

"Congratulations! I'll talk to you later."

"Roger."

After finishing the student's high work, Patten returned to the airport.

Carley had landed and left the FBO. Patten took his last student of the day and spent the hour in take-off and landing instruction. He logged in the student's time and procedures, turned her over to Linda for rescheduling, then hurried to his office and called Carley.

"How'd it go, private pilot?" he asked.

"The test went well, dear. Well…the soft-field landing wasn't too soft. There was a little gust of wind just before the main wheels touched down, and the airplane climbed, then touched down harder than I expected. I explained to the examiner what happened, and we went on for the rest of the test. He complimented both you and me, dear. He said that your students were always well trained, but that I was way above average for a 40.9-hour student! Can you believe that?" She was exuberant.

"You are way above average, babe. I'm glad he recognized it!"

"It's hard to believe that just a few weeks ago I was scared even to look at an airplane. Now the FAA thinks I'm competent enough to pilot one and carry passengers!"

"You've done very well."

"You know what, though? I'm a little sad that it's over…I mean the training with you."

"Yes, I know what you mean. I've felt the same, as I told you before. But let's get together and talk about what else we might do now."

"Yes, let's do. Will you have some time tomorrow evening?"

"Sure. Why don't you come over at about seven?"

"I'll be there."

Chapter Twenty-Two

The buzz of the intercom jolted Patten out of his reverie. "Mr. Fortis, Carley Price on line one," Linda said, sugar-sweetly.

He punched in line one. "Hi Carley," he said cheerfully. "I'm glad you—" he stopped in midsentence as he heard sniffling on the phone. "Carley, is something wrong? What's wrong?"

"Oh, Patten," Carley sobbed, openly now, "I've ruined everything!"

"What are you talking about hon, what's wrong?"

"Oh, Patten," she repeated, "Jack called, just now, just a few minutes ago—he's coming home, this afternoon! I told him our marriage was all over. But he says he wants to stay this time, that he wants to be a family man. Can you believe that!"

His heart seemed to stop. "Oh hell! Oh no, Carley!"

"Can you believe it? Can you?" she cried. "I've been so happy with you," she now sobbed uncontrollably. "Now what's going to happen to us? What? Do you realize I have an appointment with an attorney tomorrow? I was finally going to get out of this meaningless pretense of a marriage—this paper relationship. I was going to be so happy with you. Mark would have been so pleased to have you as a father!"

"Carley, don't!"

"Now that Jack's coming back I feel like such an adulteress. What have I done to myself, and to you?" she was bewildered.

"Carley, you didn't know! He didn't write, he didn't call," How were you to know?"

"But I was married. I am married!" she said, angry with herself. "Oh, I'm so confused. I don't know what to do."

"It'll take some time to sort your thoughts out about this, Carley," Patten said glumly. He tried to be supportive, but felt that the world was crashing in on him again. "Whatever you decide, I love you, and I'll be behind you. And anything you want me to do, just ask. I'll be glad to talk to Jack, if that's what you want," he said, an air of gloom settling around him.

After a long silence, Carley said, a bit more in control of herself, "Thanks. I don't know when I can talk to you again, but I'll call when I can. I love you," she said as she hung up, sobbing again.

Patten banged his hand on the desk. *Damn! That bastard has to show up! What right does he have after all this time to be a husband and father? And just when my life was turning around. Better that he was dead!* He felt a tinge of guilt for wishing Jack dead, but had little trouble dismissing that feeling.

* * *

Patten had spent a night and a day in emotional turmoil when Carley called the next evening at his duplex; she was dejected.

"I've just a minute to talk, dear. I'm in the bathroom on the cellphone. It's been so terrible!"

"How are you darling? Is Jack treating you well? It's difficult not knowing how you are, and to think about you and Jack together. I can't just call you and talk with you when I feel the need. I miss you."

"I miss you too, so very much. The difficult thing is that Jack is treating me well, very well," she cried softly. "It would be so much easier if he were nasty, if he ignored Mark and me. But he says he's been away too long, and apologized for not writing or calling. He says he loves Mark and me and will make it up to us.

"His mother is happy that he's back, and has invited us over for dinner tonight. Of course, she doesn't know you, and Jack is her only child. She's so happy to see him. He and Mark are waiting in the car for me. We're supposed to act as a happy family. He wants us to be man and wife, and I can't, I can't! Oh, this is so hard, Patten," she cried.

"I know it is, Carley…I'm so sorry that you're having to go through this," Patten said sadly. "Do you want me to talk to him? I can tell him how things are."

"I heard the door open, so I have to go. I'll call when I can. Love you," she whispered.

Patten's heart was in his stomach as he hung up the telephone. He turned on the television and stared at it while sipping a scotch and water. He thought about Carley with Jack, and Jack with Mark. When he could stand it no more, he changed into his jogging shorts and drove to the beach where he sprinted in the sand. A sharp pain in the center of his chest got his attention, but he ran faster. He ran until he was gasping for breath and could run no more. Heart pounding and soaking with sweat, he fell to the sand.

* * *

The next couple of weeks were an emotional roller coaster for Patten, and for Carley as well. Furtive short telephone calls from Carley, as she had the chance, evoked elation in Patten, followed by depression when each call ended. Patten often saw Copeland, who lent an understanding ear with intensely compassionate interest.

Chapter Twenty-Three

The telephone was ringing when Patten arrived early and unlocked the door to the FBO. His heart jumped as he recognized Carley's voice.

"I'm in the bathroom again," she laughed nervously, "and have just a moment. Jack is going to Montgomery on business and won't be back until late. Could I meet you at the FBO tonight, say 8:30? I miss you so much!"

"I miss you, too, but don't get yourself into any trouble," Patten said.

"Don't worry. It'll be okay."

"See you at 8:30 then," Patten replied, pleased that he would see her soon.

* * *

It was near noon when Chip called. "Patten, we can get that airworthiness directive completed on the one-eighty next Tuesday and Wednesday. We'll have to do it or park it—the 25 hours will be up by the time we fly over to New Orleans, you know. I'd like to go with you if you don't mind. I could use a couple of days off."

"What? Did you run out of girls around here?" Patten asked sarcastically.

Chip laughed. "There's a couple left. But I'd like to see what New Orleans has to offer."

"I'll work the trip into my schedule, Chip. You fly the airplane and I'll navigate."

"Great!"

"But remember: no heavy partying before we leave or return. The FAA says at least 12 hours from bottle to throttle."

"Hey, you may be the 'designated driver' coming back," Chip opined.

* * *

The afternoon went by slowly. Patten left the airport at six, and returned at eight o'clock. The FBO was now deserted, and he paced the floor of the lobby until Carley pulled up in the parking lot. He was waiting at the door and took her in his arms as soon as she entered. They held each other tightly for a long time, afraid to let go.

"I love you, and I've missed you so much!" Carley said, weeping on his chest.

Patten lifted her gently and carried her to the couch where he cuddled her, not wanting to speak for fear of losing the magic of having her close.

"I had a disturbing dream last night," Carley sobbed. "I dreamed I was standing alone in a desert. An airplane flew over. It was white and black. It made a rough landing. Then, I was at a flea market. I bought a small wooden rocking chair and a man whose face I never clearly saw was shopping next to me. He bought a little wooden vase. It matched my chair. It was pretty. They went together, the vase and the chair. The feeling was, well, romance, as though we would be together always, but I never saw his face. I woke up crying, upset…but I don't know why. I think the dream has something to do with us. The man's face was blank. Oh, I'm so confused," she cried.

Patten held her close, tension drawing his forehead taut, but his voice was soft. "We'll have to do something, hon: we can't go on like this." He tilted her head back to meet her eyes. "I want you to do what you want to do, what is best for you. I love you more than anything, and would be happy to be with you forever. But I realize that more than love is at stake in our situation. You have Mark to think of, and his grandmother, your friends, your husband, and your feelings about yourself.

"Mark was probably glad to see his father, and I won't encourage you to do anything that may separate them. I'm not going to ask you to go through the misery of divorce: I would blame myself for all your suffering. How could I love you and do that to you? If you were unhappy, I would be the cause."

Carley said, "Oh, I'm so confused. It's all my fault. I got—"

"No, it *isn't* all your fault," Patten interrupted. "You never twisted my arm. I was so lonely when you came along. You put something in my life that had been missing for a long time. You brought me back. You gave me something to live for, and you were lonely. We needed each other. Whatever happens, knowing you has been the high point of my life. I would not have missed it for anything, however painful it will be if I lose you."

Carley looked at him with love in her eyes. "It's hard for me to say this, but I do love you more than anything. I was so depressed, so desperate for something. I thought that Jack was never to return, but I didn't know for sure. So I wasn't free and couldn't mourn. I was caught in between, like in Purgatory, only forever. I couldn't allow myself to want to be free because that would mean Jack was dead…almost murdering him myself!

I felt guilt when I wanted to be free. Depression was all that was left for me.

"Then I met you," she went on to say, "and I began to feel again. I was no longer a robot, going through the motions of taking care of Mark, sitting at home all day, daydreaming with Jack's mother that Jack would return, which, ironically, as it turned out, he did."

After a moment of silence, Patten spoke first. "One thing that I've always loved about you, Carley," replied Patten, "is that you do such a good job of analyzing and understanding your feelings. You've taught me much about being a person."

"But it doesn't take away the pain," she countered.

"But it does relieve the confusion," he explained. "After you talk it out, then you're really not confused at all. You understand very well what has happened to you. Perhaps this is just one of the tragedies of life...no one's fault. You didn't do anything wrong, you're a good person. Some things are just beyond our control, like a microburst that you read about. But, then again, some things are just so damn tough to accept!" he ended with a surge of emotion that brought tears to his eyes.

Tears silently trickled down Carley's cheeks. Patten rested her head in the crook of his left arm while drying her tear-wet face with tissues. He noted again, as he had many times before, that she had such a beautiful face even with mascara streaking down her cheeks, and smudges around her eyes. Her now emerald eyes were sad, large and deep. *You look into her eyes, you see into her soul.* He remembered many times catching himself, as if in a trance, looking into her eyes, his thoughts suspended, and their souls meeting. "I still get lost in your eyes," he told her.

"It would be so much easier," he eventually said, "if Jack were different, as you said. If he were a wife beater, a child hater, or just irresponsible...but he's not. He's had trouble settling down, I suppose.

You're certainly not as close to him as you are to me. You can't talk with him as well about feelings and problems because he's not that type of person. But maybe he's trying, and does what he can, which is all that you can really ask of anyone. And you're married to him. I won't ask you to leave him for me. If you ever decide that you're unhappy with him, though, I want to be the first in line."

"Oh, I wish it were only a question of love," Carley said, momentarily more concerned about Patten's anguish than her own. She ran her right hand across his cheek to the back of his head, and tenderly pulled his head down to kiss him.

He understood her concern for him, and was filled with warmth for her again, as he had been many times before—for her kindness and concern for him. "It tears my heart out to think of losing you," he said, choked with emotion. "But I can't get on with my life with our relationship as it is. I have to make a decision, hon. I think of you most of the day, everyday.

"I can't call you because I don't know who'll answer the telephone. You don't have the opportunity to call me often. I worry about you, whether you and Mark are well, whether you're doing okay. If you needed me, how would I know?" he asked, thinking out loud.

"Dear," said Carley, "Something will happen for us. I don't know what. It's difficult for both of us. You're with me all the time. I see something in every room of the house that reminds me of you. I have the first gift that you gave me in my bedroom, and other gifts, and books and toys that you bought for Mark in every room of my house. I can't live without you, because you're my love and my very best friend. I'm able to talk to you about everything," she said.

They sat silently for a time, each realizing that the issue had been approached but skirted, and that it would have to be faced at some point. The sound of tires rolling over gravel and headlights shining through the windows alerted them to the approach of a car pulling into the parking lot. Carley and Patten separated and rose from the couch.

"Will you call me next Thursday morning at ten o'clock?" she asked. "Mark and I will be home alone. Jack is going gulf fishing."

"Sure," Patten said as he unlocked the door and watched her to her car. He recognized an airplane owner who had pulled into the parking lot and was making his way across the ramp to his airplane.

Patten locked the door to the FBO, entered his car and left the airport. He stopped at a supermarket and picked up a six-pack of beer, drove to his favorite place to think on the beach, and sat on the sand sipping beer and watching the waves.

He had a gut feeling that Carley was gone from his life, at least as someone to love and from whom to receive love. He knew what he had to do, but could he bring himself to do it? A close friendship would be the best relationship, he thought, although he wanted more. He didn't want to hurt Carley. He didn't want her to feel rejected. He wasn't at all sure that a love relationship could be turned into a close friend relationship, although the reverse often happened.

As he sat on the white sand and watched the waves cresting and foaming, he missed Carley very much. He wished she were present. He felt a moment of anger that Jack would leave her and go on a fishing trip, or go to South America or Saudi Arabia for adventure, while Patten would fly around the world, if necessary, to spend a few hours with her. Jack took her for granted. He had her to come home to when he wished. He really didn't need her. He didn't understand her or enjoy her. He couldn't cope with her feelings, although he had probably coped with many things in life.

When Patten glanced at his watch in the moonlight, he saw that it was already 2:30. He arose feeling tired and heavy, and drove back to the duplex.

Chapter Twenty-Four

The following Tuesday morning, Patten met Chip at the airport and filed an instrument flight plan for 4,000 feet direct to Brookley airway intersection in Mobile, then Victor Airway 198-240 to Pearl intersection, followed by Victor 240 to Lakefront Airport in New Orleans. Chip took the left seat, and Patten handled the radio from the right seat and gave navigation instruction. They departed Gulf Shores Aviation at 7:00 a.m. in the Cherokee one-eighty with an ETA of 8:45 a.m. at Lakefront.

Patten dozed but checked Chip's heading every 15 minutes and handled the radio traffic. Halfway into the flight, Chip's speech began dragging, appeared drowsy, and he was having trouble maintaining altitude and heading.

"Chip, do you think you need some glucose?"

"Guess so," Chip lazily responded. "Suppose I should've had some breakfast this morning, after my shot."

Patten took the controls while Chip found the glucose tablets in his overnight bag, and popped a couple.

In a few moments Chip was back to his alert self, and reclaimed the controls. He was happy and relaxed at the controls until, 20 miles east of

Lakefront, the one-eighty entered a cloudbank. Chip gave it a try, but couldn't maintain course and altitude. He needed to see the horizon as a visual reference since he had never had any instrument training. Patten took over as the airplane banked 60 degrees and was losing altitude. "I'll give you a rest, now," Patten said.

Patten wasn't cleared to descend for a radar-vectored instrument approach to runway 36 Right until he was almost over the airport. The parallel runways of Lakefront jutted out into Lake Pontchartrain, and he didn't treasure the thought of running off the end of the short runway into the lake. He dove and intercepted the ILS signal, but was too high. At 300 feet, just when he was ready to declare a missed approach, he broke out of the stratus and side-slipped the airplane to quickly lose altitude for the landing.

Chip taxied back to the FBO, and they left the Cherokee in the hands of the mechanics. They were told the aircraft would be ready at 6 p.m. the following day.

Loading their luggage into a taxi outside the gate, they headed for the Sheraton.

"You're welcome to share the room and tab with me tonight," Patten said.

"Thanks, but no thanks," Chip said lightheartedly, "since you're not my type. I think I can do better. Anyway, man, you've been down for some reason the last few days and would be no fun. Too, there's a beautiful woman out there, somewhere, who's going to invite me to share a room with her for free, and I don't think we'll be doing much sleeping."

"Suit yourself," Patten said. "But the room at the Sheraton is safer."

"No, man, I'm careful. I may die of exhaustion, but not from sexual disease. If I can't find a condom, I'll grab a sandwich bag or plastic wrap from the kitchen, or something. Anyway, as you know, I fool around only with nice girls."

Patten had to grin. "Any girl you fool around with is, ipso facto, not a nice girl. Those are not virgins you're sleeping with, you know!"

"Come on, you insult me, Patten. My girls may not be exactly virgins, but they are only slightly used. They have to be charmed, manipulated, and convinced to give in. They don't sleep with every Tom, Dick, and Harry that comes along."

At the Sheraton, Patten checked in, and Chip had the bell desk attendant hold his luggage for him until later in the day.

When they stepped out the door into the street, the air was heavy and low stratus clouds hung over the city. It was approaching noon but the city was not yet up. Patten's stomach reminded him that he hadn't had breakfast, and Chip's hands were trembling.

Three blocks from the Sheraton, they passed a small restaurant that, on a sign in the front window, proudly proclaimed: "Cajun Cooking— Best in Town." Chip peeked in the window, and a white-uniformed, perky looking waitress caught his eye. "Looks promising," Chip said as they walked in.

"Hi," Chip called out, as the waitress turned toward them from the table she was cleaning. She was tall and slender. Her straight black hair and bangs outlined a china-doll looking face.

"Hello," she smiled. She waved the two of them over to her. "Ready for lunch? Come and have a seat, I'm just finishing with this table."

"Well, I don't think I'm ready for any serious Cajun cooking yet. Just got in town, and haven't had breakfast," Chip smiled back at her as he sat down. "How about coffee with cream? And can I get a Danish roll in this Cajun town?"

"Sure," she said, "raspberry, lemon, or chocolate?"

"Raspberry will do."

She smiled at Patten as he took a seat, "and what would you have?"

"I'll have the same," he said, as he settled in to watch the performance.

"Coming up," she said as she walked toward the kitchen.

"You may need some extra insulin this morning, Chip, if you're going to eat that sweet roll."

"Maybe. I'll see how I feel after I level out. But look at that figure, Patten. My search for the New Orleans beauty may have ended already!"

"Poor girl," Patten said, good-naturedly.

"Pay attention, man. You may learn something."

"About some things, I'd rather stay ignorant."

China doll returned quickly with steaming cups of coffee. "Sweet rolls will be heated in a minute," she said, beaming again. She busied herself rearranging the salt and pepper shakers. "Not much of a breakfast," she said, with manufactured concern in her voice.

"I'll make up for it later," Chip said. "We don't get by here very often—any recommendations for dinner? I like seafood."

"Well, I love seafood, too," she said. "New Orleans is noted for its seafood, you know," she was thoughtful for moment. "Blake's Port O'Call is about the best around. Medium priced." She hurried back to the kitchen, sliding her hand along her hip as she walked.

"Bingo," Chip said.

She returned with hot rolls, knives and forks, and placed them on the table. She then wiped a cloth around the already spotless table. She smiled prettily again. "Blake's is off the beaten path. Are you familiar with New Orleans?"

"Let's introduce ourselves. I'm Chip Summers, and this is Patten Fortis. We flew in this morning to Lakefront Airport to have some work done on an airplane. I've been here two or three times before, but I don't know my way around. I'll be here until tomorrow evening," he seemed to chat easily within the coded message framework, which, however, was so transparent everyone clearly understood. "Don't know where I'll be staying yet—Patten is staying at the Sheraton, and he has some plans for the night. I left my luggage over at the Sheraton." He took a bite of his roll and a sip of coffee.

"I'm glad to meet you guys! My name is Sally...Sally Majors," she said. "I'll be back in a minute." She left to make rounds of the other tables occupied by a few customers, filled their coffee cups, and quickly returned. "How's the sweet roll?"

"Very good," Chip said. Patten nodded in agreement.

"Made them myself, fresh this morning," she said playfully.

"Not only a good waitress, but a good cook too!" Chip played along.

"You bet. A woman of many talents," she flirted.

"Well, Sally, woman of many talents, could you tell me if you know a good-looking waitress who lies about her cooking skills that might show me how to find Blake's in exchange for dinner, at about eight o'clock tonight?"

She looked at him in delight. "I know of one," she said, "but she wouldn't be ready until nine o'clock. She's worth waiting for, though!"

"Sheraton lobby at 9:30?" he inquired.

Sally nodded agreement, smiled and left to again make rounds of the other customers.

Having finished his hot rolls and coffee, Patten shook his head at Chip. "On that note, I think I'll leave. I'm the odd one out here. Why don't you stick around, practice your charm, and then pay the bill?" he suggested. "Looks like you won't be among the homeless tonight."

"Sure, it's my turn," Chip grinned. "Meet you back at the Sheraton at five tomorrow?"

A TIME IN THE SUN

"See you then," Patten replied. "But until I see you again, there is one question I want you to ponder: Who is the one picked up here?" Patten asked, then started back to the hotel.

* * *

Patten awoke from a nap at eight p.m. according to the digital clock on the nightstand. He showered, put on a fresh shirt and socks and left the Sheraton to find dinner. It was cooler now than earlier in the day, but the ceiling was still low and a drizzle fell intermittently. The humidity was so high that Patten felt he could wash his hands in the air if he had any soap. He walked over to the French Quarter, and though he was not hungry found a quiet restaurant where he treated himself to a dinner of sole almandine. Then he braved the gathering crowds that was bringing the Quarter to life, and aimlessly strode around. He hardly noticed the hawkers along the doorways or the half-nude girl swinging on a rope out the window of a club. He walked around for two hours through the faceless crowd before he returned to the Sheraton.

But at the door of the hotel he decided he could not bear the loneliness of the motel room so he continued down the street. At the end of Canal Street he took an elevator to the revolving restaurant-lounge at the top of the World Trade Mart. He picked up a Chivas and water at the bar in the center, and sat at a window table.

A kaleidoscope of lights reflected off the low clouds, which were pierced here and there by scattered spires of the city. Below, he could clearly see the river and reflections of light off the water. The city was alive, vibrant. The vista would have been a very pleasant one had his mind not been so heavy. As it was, he felt insignificant, small, an observer of life rather than a part of life itself. In a word, he was lonely, again.

He did understand what he wanted: he wanted Carley. He wanted to be with her, to love her, to laugh with her, to learn from her perceptiveness of him, his needs, thoughts, strengths and weaknesses, to nurture her in her pain and to be nurtured by her in his pain. But most of all, he could not bare to hurt her. He had rather give her up than to make her life difficult.

Then he felt sick with himself. Was he really sacrificing himself to save Carley from pain, or did he want to avoid guilt by not hurting her. Was his motive selfish or generous? Was he still merely acting out a role his mother had prepared for him years ago? He had no answer—perhaps there was none. The question was moot, anyway, because his action would have to be the same regardless of his motive, he decided.

Carley received little from Jack, yet she was married to him and felt the obligation to be his wife even if she had to sacrifice her own needs. She would feel like a heel to leave this man, that's the kind of person she is, he thought, and regardless of the fact that Jack and Carley had no relationship, he could not interfere with her attempt to make the marriage work. She can't make the decision to let me go, so it's best for her and for me, that I step out of the picture, he thought.

He had never made any critical comments about Jack to Carley and never would because he knew that any observation he made would be tainted by his own needs, for one thing and, for another, any criticism of Jack would make her task to achieve marital harmony more difficult. After thinking it over, he believed that Carley's marriage was a hopeless one since she and her husband were such different people and didn't love each other, but he would not deliver the coup de grace. Carley must be given room to try her best, he thought.

How would he get over her? Ending a relationship in anger, he'd heard someone say, is easier than ending one in depression, since anger allowed the rejection of the other person. He considered every mannerism, every facet of her being, to try and find a defect, an Achilles' heel, something that would lessen her status in his eyes, but he could think of none. Soon the threat of guilt entering his consciousness ended that search. How could he try to find fault in her, merely to make separation easier for himself?

Why the anger toward Carley, he asked himself? She had done nothing to him, had she? The obvious answer, of course, is that she had not divorced Jack and married him. Yet, he was most comfortable leaving that decision up to Carley. However, he was aware of feeling anger toward her all the same.

He saw, in his mind's eye, as he had done hundreds of times before, Dr. Copeland sitting across from him and listening attentively. He imagined the psychologist regarding him kindly, encouraging Patten to dig deeper, to follow the feeling to its source. *I feel resentment toward her…because…because…I love her so much. She seems to have control over me. I feel good when she's near, bad when she's away. Good when she calls, bad when I don't hear from her. I'm so dependent on her for how I feel! I think I'm angry at her because I feel so dependent on her! I resent the resulting control she has over my feelings. That would be humorous in a way, if it weren't so painful, Dr. Copeland. The short answer then, is that I love her so much I resent her! And, of course, she doesn't deserve any of this anger or resentment. I wonder if all deep love relationships have such tangled emotions!*

Although he felt he had more of a handle on his feelings, he nevertheless sat brooding through three more drinks, dreading yet knowing that he would have to end the relationship. Returning to his vacant room—to his cold bed—he ended the evening in loneliness.

* * *

His night of erratic sleep, as usual it seemed, was filled with disturbing dreams. He awoke as the first rays of dawn filtered through the bedroom curtains, and lay half awake realizing he had been dreaming of Carley. He remembered a scene in which he, Carley and Jack were together. Her husband angrily described to Patten Carley's shortcomings, and Carley tried to get him to stop. Carley was pregnant. Then, in the very next scene, he was in Carley's house to spend the night. When he walked into the bedroom and turned on the light, spiders scattered everywhere. He was not afraid, although with each step he took, spiders scurried out of the carpet. He decided that he could not sleep in the room with all the spiders about and pondered whether to tell Carley why he could not sleep there. He was concerned, though, that her feelings would be hurt, that she may think he regarded her as a poor housekeeper. He knew that she did keep a clean house, and if she knew the insects were there, she would certainly have exterminators out. But he took another look at the spiders, knew that he could not sleep there and decided that he would have to tell her, would have to make her understand in a way that her feelings would be spared.

Patten finally arose and dressed in an exercise suit and tennis shoes. After jogging 30 minutes through the streets of the still-sleeping city, he returned to his room, showered and dressed. Feeling thereby refreshed, he ate a leisurely continental breakfast, and sat in the atrium to relax and read the morning newspaper. Prominent on front page was an article of an interview with federal and state officials who were afraid the city would be hit by a level four or five hurricane this season, and that the levees would not be sufficient to protect the city.

Returning to his room, he packed his luggage and checked out. The bell clerk agreed to hold his luggage until five o'clock. Thus unburdened, Patten took a stroll along the river walk, an enclosed walkway that paralleled the river. He stopped to browse in the many shops along the way and at one point was tempted to try one of the fortunetellers. He needed something to look forward to, some hope for the future.

A couple of Coney islands at three o'clock got him through the afternoon, and he returned to the lobby of the Sheraton to await Chip.

Chip showed up a few minutes later, and appeared hung-over.

"You don't look so happy, Chip. Come on over and tell me how it went," Patten said.

Chip sat down. "It was great," he said.

"Well, come on, what happened?" Patten insisted.

"Okay, okay, Patten. Sally met me as she said she would yesterday. We had a great dinner at Blake's—you should try it next time you're here—then we returned here and picked up my luggage. The little girl was a tiger. When I woke up this morning my body felt as though it had been through a meat grinder. I'll tell you what, Patten, that was serious sex—going to take me some time to recuperate. I'm going to be down for maintenance for a few days!" he said dramatically.

"Sally was gone this morning when I woke up. She left a note on the bed sheet. It said, 'wasn't that worth waiting for?' and she left the telephone number for the restaurant. I called her up and said, 'yes.' She said 'thanks for the dinner, the company, and everything else.' She apologized that she had been deprived a long time and took it out on me. She invited me to eat a hearty breakfast at the restaurant, which I did, and to discuss an encore performance, which I didn't. Forgive the pun, Patten, but I didn't feel 'up' to it."

Patten chuckled, "Now come on, Chip, you're not going to tell me this was the best you ever had? You always say that after each binge."

"You're asking a serious question at a weak moment for me, Patten, and so I don't have the strength to tell you a lie." He thought for a minute, and then said, "To be honest, that appendage of mine has a very short memory," whereupon they both laughed.

"Another thing, though," Chip went on, more seriously "and this is embarrassing: I really didn't enjoy myself that much. I don't know what's happening to me. In the midst of drinking and sex, I began to feel that something was lacking—that there ought to be more to a relationship than this. You meet a girl, soon you're in bed having sex. Then you separate and that's it! It's more of an encounter than anything else. Nothing you would call 'making love.'"

"I think I know what you mean, Chip."

"And," Chip added, now in a somber tone, "I worry about how much longer this tool of mine is going to work."

"Because of the diabetes mellitus?"

"Yeah." After a short pause, Chip then thought out loud: "I wonder if that saying is right?"

"What saying?"

"If you don't use it, you lose it."

"Is that what's been driving you? Maybe if you overuse it, you lose it!"

They took a taxi and arrived at Lakefront by six o'clock. The service manager was gone for the day, and a lineman led Patten and Chip to the maintenance hangar. There they were pointed toward a black-headed, greasy-looking mechanic whose temples jutted out toward unruly eyebrows. Oily, black hair stood out from his collar and shirtsleeves. He had ingrained grease in the pores and wrinkles of his skin and embedded under his fingernails; the mechanic looked as though he had taken a bath in motor oil. His face was covered with acne, at least the part you could see through the grease and three-day stubble. No matter how much he showers, Patten thought, he probably still looks greasy.

"An embarrassment to the profession," Chip said under his breath to Patten.

"We're here to pick up the Cherokee one-eighty," he said to the mechanic.

"Oh, yeah," the hirsute mechanic coughed and cleared his throat. He left and momentarily returned with the bill and airplane maintenance logbook. "We didn't find any corrosion, and completion of the AD has been entered into the logbook." He handed Patten a bill covered with black smudges. "You can take this to the cashier in the office and pick up your key."

Patten paid the bill, after having the lineman top off the one-eighty, while Chip inspected underneath the wings to insure that the fuel bladders, which had to be removed to perform the inspection, were not leaking. The visibility was only one mile and the ceiling was low at 700 feet when Patten filed an instrument flight plan for 5,000 feet in reverse sequence from their route into Lakefront.

"And when is the airplane most dangerous to fly, Master Mechanic?" He asked Chip.

Chip grinned. "Right after maintenance, of course! Let's give it a good going over before we start up."

After satisfying themselves that the one-eighty was airworthy, they departed runway 36 Right, with Chip in control. Climbing out over Lake Pontchartrain, the gray mist enveloped the airplane at 700 feet. Patten squelched the strobe and landing lights. He took control from Chip and made a right turn on course, as directed by the air traffic controller.

The Cherokee broke out of the thick stratus layer at 4,000 feet, and

Patten clicked the strobes back on. With the star-swept clear night above and a smooth carpet of stratus below, Chip took over and flew without incident to Gulf Shores Aviation.

Chapter Twenty-Five

The next morning he was up and showered by the time his alarm clock went off at seven o'clock. He dressed and stopped by Bogart's for a light breakfast more out of habit than hunger. Caffeine put some life in him, and he drove on to the airport.

A dream from the night before stuck in his mind. In the dream he was sleeping with Carley. Aroused from his sleep, he sees that Carley has arisen and is walking around the room. She is mumbling, but Patten understands that she is saying she must go and clean the shower room. She is sleepwalking, and Patten knows that she should not be awakened.

He follows her to the shower room, where several men are taking showers. She vacuums water from the floor. The men are surprised to see her and start to say that she doesn't belong there, but Patten shushes them with a finger to his lips.

She completes the vacuuming, and Patten leads her back to bed without awakening her. He doesn't know whether he should tell her, when she awakens, of what she has done. He feels that somehow she would be hurt if he told her.

He was still pondering the meaning of the dream when he pulled into the parking lot of Gulf Shores Aviation. Linda was not in as yet. Patten unlocked the door, turned on the lights, and checked his schedule. He had no flight instruction until eleven o'clock. He wished he were busy so that he could focus his mind on something to distract him from his pain. He took out the accounts payable folder from the file, went into the office and shut the door. He began writing checks to his suppliers—Gasser Banners in Nashville, AVMAT in Memphis, Gulf Telephone, Phillips Oil Company—he disliked having bills to pay but he always felt relieved to pay them, to balance the account as it were, to discharge obligations, to gain relief from one of the many burdens lurking in the back of his mind.

As he finished writing checks for the bills, he heard Linda arrive. He was glad his door was closed, as he didn't feel up to small talk.

He punched in Carley's number at exactly ten o'clock. She was waiting for his call. The telephone rang only once.

"Hello," her voice broke—the tension obvious.

"Hi," he tried to be casual.

She rambled, launching into a seemingly endless account of the night and morning's events with Mark, breakfast, and housecleaning. Noticeably absent was any mention of Jack. Patten was trying to figure out what point she was trying to make, when it dawned on him that she was saying the safe and insignificant to delay the painful and significant.

"Carley...Carley, shut up, babe," he gently interrupted.

"What?" she asked. "Why aren't you saying anything? I think this is going to be bad. It is, isn't it?"

"Carley," he managed to say, "if I didn't love you so much I could probably go on with our relationship as it is forever. But now that Jack is back, you're very uncomfortable with our relationship. We can't talk as much, and you're afraid of getting caught with me. You're a married woman again, for sure, and you're not the type of person to be married to one man and to love another.

"But I can't go on like this. I live you everyday. If I see you, I'm happy—if we have one of our long talks, I'm pleased. But then after three hours or so away from you, I miss you and need to see you again. Ordinary flying no longer takes my mind off you. I think about you when I'm instructing and really don't know if I'm doing my students justice. I can't seem to get on with my life, whatever that is, but then again, I can't imagine my life without you. I can't think of Patten post-Carley!"

She became hysterical. "I understand that you want to get rid of me!" Carley sobbed, hurt and anger in her voice. "Is there someone else?"

Patten was astonished that he was so falsely accused. "Wait a minute, Carley! You don't know what you're saying."

As her sobbing grew louder, Patten grew softer: "I'm trying to say, Carley, that I love you. It's painful to love you and not to have you, and to have to share you with someone else, not to be able to see you or talk to you or share my feelings with you or to hear yours or to know that you and Mark are okay."

Carley was crying more softly now. "I was so down when I met you. I was alone and needed you, and I need you now. I can't bear to think that I can't pick up the phone and call you or race down to the airport to see you when I need you."

"Carley, dear, it's you who have saved me. I had the love part of myself anesthetized. You allowed me to love again, gave me a purpose to live, helped me to understand myself and understand you and other people. You shared Mark with me. I'll always be here for you if you need me, and I'll always be your best friend."

"I'll never hear from you again!" she cried. "I know how these things turn out. It's a way of letting someone down easily, saying you want to be friends."

"Listen, Carley, we're not teenagers, we have a lot invested in each other. I don't want to give all that up. I mean what I say and I want you to believe me. I want to know how things go with you. But we must not talk of love again—it would open a flood of troubling feelings in me."

"I'm sorry, forgive me, of course I believe you. Sometimes I say stupid things," Carley said, then sobbing again, "Oh, I've messed everything up as I always do, and I do want you to be happy, I do!"

"No. You did nothing wrong, Carley. You had every reason to believe that Jack would never be involved with you and Mark. If you had known he was coming back, I know we would not have ever become involved. It's circumstances beyond your control, a tragedy, that's all."

She fell silent for a moment, and then said, "I don't know what's wrong with me. I do know that you love me. I know you wouldn't hurt me, and I love you. Sometimes I think that Jack doesn't even like me. He criticizes me and wants to change me. You love me, I think, for what I am, and if Jack does love me, it's not for what I am but for what he thinks I can become. Does that make sense? Do you understand?"

"You're so wise," he said with great conviction and emotion. "It's such a waste that he doesn't know you and doesn't know how to enjoy you. It's so sad!" Then feeling guilty for having criticized Jack and maybe making things worse for Carley, he added, "But he needs you in some way. He's not such a bad person; it's just that you and he are different. Maybe you two will develop a better relationship."

Carley was now upset again. She again became hysterical, and in a shrill, plaintive voice, she warned, "You'll look but you won't find anyone else like me. I'm the one for you. I understand you better than anyone else!"

Patten agreed, subdued both by the truth of the prediction and the pain he heard enmeshed in the words. "Yes, yes, I know you're right," he said quietly, and then he was at a loss for further words.

He heard her crying softly in the silence that followed. Knowing nothing else to offer if he were to remain resolute, he eventually said, "Bye Carley, I'll talk to you later," and hung up when she did not reply. He hoped she would be all right—he didn't know any other way to do it. He was more concerned at that time with her than with himself, but he knew that as the day wore on, his own pain would demand more attention.

* * *

Patten flew for an hour with a student, and then returned to the FBO. Upon entering the lobby, Linda called to him. She held the telephone in her hand. "It's Carley Price," she said, rolling her eyes.

"You really should have your eyes checked, Linda," he said coldly.

He rushed to his office and grabbed the phone.

"Hello, Carley," he said.

"I won't be bothering you all the time with telephone calls," she said. "I know I haven't had much time for you lately with Jack home," she sighed. "I'm so stupid!" she said angrily. "I'm afraid I've lost you. I don't know how you've put up with me this long," she sobbed.

"Carley, don't. There's nothing wrong with you, its just circumstances," Patten said.

"You'll do so much better than me," she cried. "I feel like such a big baby!"

He chose to be silent although his returning anguish pushed for expression.

After a few minutes, Carley said, "I know you're busy, I'll let you get back to work...I do want you to be happy. I won't bother you with a lot of calls."

"Call anytime, Carley," he said sadly as he hung up the phone. He hated himself for being so trite and distant but he knew nothing else to say or do.

He closed the door to his office, as the emptiness and ache in his stomach and chest became almost unbearable. He felt better to place his arms across his stomach and double over. He wept silently for a few minutes, then gathered himself together and buzzed Linda on the intercom.

"Linda, cancel my appointments today. I'll be out the rest of the day."

"All of them?" she asked, baffled.

"Yes. I do plan to be here tomorrow, though."

Linda stared at him quizzically as he left his office and walked by the counter. He hoped she did not see his eyes behind the sunglasses.

He turned up the radio as he drove down Highway 59 South toward the duplex. But the radio was his enemy. Every song of love and problems in love relationships brought fresh anguish to him and a surge of pain in his stomach. He turned the radio off and screamed, again and again, until he finally found some curious relief.

It's a good thing no one can hear me, he reflected, or I'd be put in a straight jacket and hauled off to the nearest psychiatric ward. At the time, though, he didn't care very much one way or the other.

At the duplex, he lay in bed trying to sleep, but sleep would not come although his eyes felt full of sand. When he was finally not able to tolerate his thoughts any longer, he changed into shorts and drove to the beach at the state resort.

He left his shoes in the car and walked west along the beach, under the fishing pier, and in front of the condos, beach houses, and motels. He was unmindful of the sensation of water rushing over his feet, or of tourists passing on the beach. Lost in his thoughts he actually bumped into a couple walking hand in hand. Deep sadness welled up in him again, and he suddenly sprinted down the beach as if to try to distance himself from the pain. His toes dug into the sand with each step. His breathing became labored and his heart pounded in his ears. As he neared exhaustion, thoughts of death crossed his mind and lent him a sort of inexplicable respite.

Pain began in his upper legs and chest and when he was exhausted, he collapsed on the sand and lay there heaving, finally relieved that the demands of his body drew attention away from his mental loss: physical pain was much easier to bear than emotional pain.

Chapter Twenty-Six

Patten was towing along the coast a restaurant advertising banner, "STEAK & LOBSTER AT THE POINT" when it happened. The Cherokee suddenly shuddered and yawed to the left. Patten quickly stomped in the right rudder, but looking out at the left wing saw rivets popping and sheet metal separating. He swiftly pulled the tow release lever, dropping the banner into the Gulf, and just as quickly throttled back.

His efforts were in vain. The port wing separated from the fuselage and fell toward the Gulf. Lift on the remaining wing spun the aircraft counterclockwise and nose down until it plunged with a splash into the greenish-blue water.

* * *

Mark was playing in the den while Carley was drying dishes in the kitchen when a news bulletin flashed in on the TV. Carley walked to the door of the den with a plate in one hand and drying towel in the other. She caught part of the broadcast: "…crashed into the Gulf some 1500 yards offshore in the vicinity of Orange Beach. The airplane was pulling an advertising banner, when, witnesses reported, a wing came off. Watch for details on the six o'clock news."

"Oh, my God!" she exclaimed, as she hurried to the telephone and dialed Gulf Shores Aviation.

"Linda, this is Carley Price. Is Patten in?"

"Hold on a minute," Linda said tightly.

Moments later, the telephone clicked: "Mrs. Price, Leland Robertson. I'm sorry, but Patten is not here. Could I help you?"

Carley lost it. She screamed into the phone: "Where is he? I just heard that an airplane towing a banner crashed into the Gulf! Is he flying banners today?"

Leland waited a moment, trying his best to be diplomatic: "Yes, we've had people calling in and reporting a crash. We hope it wasn't Patten, but he was flying a banner and we haven't heard from him. He's been gone over two hours. A woman called, described the color of the airplane and said it was a low-wing airplane. I don't know anyone else around who uses a low wing aircraft to tow banners. Looks bad," he said grimly.

"Oh...no!" Carley cried.

"A boat was nearby, and a body was pulled from the sinking fuselage. We're waiting on the authorities to identify the body," he said sadly.

Carley hung up the phone, sobbing hysterically. She knew in her heart that Patten was dead. Mark ran to his mother and began crying, not knowing what was wrong but afraid because his mother was upset.

On the nightly news witnesses described the crash, and a tourist showed the scene he had captured of the short drama on a video camera. Carley watched in horror as she saw the port wing tear off, and the fuselage and starboard wing roll over and spin into the water.

***

"I know what the National Transportation Safety Board will say after they finish their investigation," Chip told Leland disgustedly, as they sipped coffee in the pilot's lounge. Mimicking an imaginary NTSB spokesperson, he said: "After an extensive investigation, the NTSB found that the left wing spar had broken at the fuselage, the left wing had therefore deplaned and the aircraft spun out of control. Probable cause of the deplaning was weakness of the wing spar due to damage incurred during the process of an earlier required inspection. The pilot, Patten Fortis, a pilot with more than 4,000 hours pilot-in-command time, was fatally injured in the resulting crash.

"In light of this accident and findings of other wing spars weakened by the required inspection, along with the fact that no inspected aircraft were found to have corrosion of a significant degree in their wing spars, the A.D. was amended to apply only to those aircraft in question which had logged more than 15,000 hours in low-level, turbulent flight."

"You're undoubtedly right, Chip," Leland said, exasperated. "Ironic, isn't it? The inspection itself caused more danger than the corrosion it was supposed to reveal and correct!"

***

Light rain was falling as Carley arrived at the memorial service for Patten. Fellow pilots, flight students, and employees of Gulf Shores Aviation were invited to the ceremony. Leland had designed a plaque to be hung in the flight instruction room at Gulf Shores Aviation in Patten's honor, as the instructor who had organized the flight school.

Carley's cheeks were red from irritation caused by the constant dabbing at tears with tissues. Her eyes were red and swollen.

She was lost in her thoughts and didn't hear what was being said as she sat alone in a pew as the owner of the FBO, flight instructors and former students related their experiences and feelings about Patten. She didn't take the opportunity to speak, believing that she would not be able to keep her composure, and really, she could only share with others her experience with flight instructor Patten, and nothing about the, to her, much more valuable loving relationship they had enjoyed together.

"I wonder if, the more the love, the greater the pain," Patten had said. All in all, though, she was glad she had this period of joy in her life. And she felt Patten was not entirely gone from her life.

After the service, Carley was returning to her car when Chip called to her: "Carley...Carley Price?"

"Yes?" she answered, as she recognized the approaching man as an airplane mechanic she had seen around the airport. The man was with Rose, a flight instructor that had taught Carley ground school on a few occasions. She had heard that the woman divorced, and the mechanic and flight instructor were now engaged.

Chip, carrying a small box, left Rose and approached Carley. "Hi. I'm Chip Summers, an aircraft mechanic at the airport. We've never been introduced, but I know you were a student of Patten's. When we went through his desk we found this box with your name on it. It's yours—something he wanted you to have," he said, as he handed the box to her. "Also, Patten left a letter for Leland, the owner of the FBO, requesting that his ashes be scattered off the Gulf coast if anything happened to him. I wondered if you'd like to do that. If you don't feel up to it, I can get Rose or one of the other flight instructors..."

"Oh, no," Carley interrupted. "I'll be glad to do it...and thank you!"

"Good. You can pick up the urn from Leland," Chip said. He turned to walk away, but then turned back.

"Patten never talked about you, Mrs. Price," he said compassionately. "But he was never a happy, or even contented, man before you came to the airport. A person would have had to be blind not to see the change in him after he began giving you flight lessons. Before he met you, he seemed preoccupied with personal problems, maybe bad experiences, and he wasn't very close to anyone at the airport so he never talked about personal things, or about his past. He worked, treated people fairly, paid his bills, and tried to be the best pilot and flight instructor he could be. That was the sum total of his life as I knew it. After you came along, he began to enjoy himself. He smiled. He laughed. He talked. You were very special to him. You helped him find the only happiness I've ever seen him have. I want you to know I'm thankful that you happened along," he smiled as he shook her hand.

"Thank you," she said, her voice fatigued and thin, as she fought back more tears while Chip left her and returned to Rose.

Carley sat in her car and with trembling hands tore the tape off the small box. Inside, she found an envelope addressed to her, and a silver-colored replica of a Cessna one fifty-two on a stand. "TO CARLEY" was imprinted on the base. The "N" number of the one fifty-two she had trained in was stamped on the fuselage of the replica.

She carefully opened the envelope and took out a cassette. Nervously she inserted a switch key, turned on the radio, and pushed in the cassette. At once she identified Patten's calm, flight-instructor voice:

"Hi Love:

"You wouldn't be listening to this tape if something hadn't happened to me. I've told you that the most dangerous part of an airplane trip is the drive to and from the airport. But airplane accidents also happen. I've had fleeting images as well as dreams of being in an airplane, tumbling out of control through the sky. I am not terrified in these visions and dreams. In fact, what I feel at these times is more like serenity—a joining with or encounter with my fate, 'if that makes any sense,' as you used to say.

"Anyway, I asked myself what I wished to say to you if I had only one other opportunity; thus this tape.

"Since I met you, Carley, I've had fulfillment in my life. Before I met you I existed, but was emotionally sterile. You brought me the color, the love, the intimacy that had been lacking. I had been so very lonely and did not realize it until you came along. I've loved you more deeply than I ever imagined I could love anyone. At the same time, I felt love from you. The sharing of love with you has been pure joy. The happiest moments of my life have been with you. Life would have been incomplete without you.

"I don't know that much about life, Carley, but I've heard that our fears and experiences beginning in early childhood build walls around our possibilities and interfere with our relationships as we go through life. You don't recognize the walls until you bump into them over and over again as life goes on. Sometimes people help you to recognize those walls. The walls are not all bad; there is security behind those walls, but they become stifling. Flying for me has been something of an escape from those enclosures. I soared above the walls, and found relief, but it was always momentary. Carley, hon, you played a large part in helping me to confront, cope with, and resolve some of the issues from which those walls were built, and I found that same happiness and freedom on land with you.

"Those walls kept me depressed, honey. I am sure I had a death wish after those painful experiences I lived through. I took too many chances, was too reckless in my flying when I was alone. Then I met you, and that death wish became a life wish, a wish to live and a burning desire to be with you. You fulfilled my life.

"Darling, I know that you understand why I had to let you go. To continue on would have been selfish of me. I couldn't stand for you to be torn between your feelings for me and what you saw as your responsibilities, and I didn't want to interfere with any chance you had for reconciliation in your marriage. How could I live with the feeling that I made you unhappy? So I distanced myself from you. Of course, I knew you would hurt for me to let you go, but I hoped the hurt would not last forever. And I hoped that my hurt would not last forever. Forgive me for any pain I caused you.

"As for me, my heart felt as though it was being wrenched from my chest to let you go. Today, as I record this, it has been 63 days since I last saw you and Mark. Each of those days I missed you terribly. It was almost intolerable. I sometimes thought I saw the back of your head in a crowd, and I hurried to overtake you, to once again catch a glimpse of you, but each time the woman turned out to be a stranger. Each day, an incident…a song…a voice…reminded me of you. I would find myself in the middle of a sentence, a thought of you would flash through my mind, and I'd forget what I was saying. It has been almost impossible to think of life after us, but I've tried to go on, building on the promise of our relationship—the promise that life can be better. There was no promise before we met."

Carley stopped the tape for a moment to wipe at her eyes, and then continued playing.

"I want to tell you to please not mourn for me, but knowing you, I understand that's not possible. So I hope you'll let yourself mourn for a short time, but then get over it! I'll be with you always, as you'll be with me. Go ahead with your life, whatever you choose to do with it. I'll be pleased.

"I hope you'll continue flying—you're a natural pilot! And when you're flying along above the clouds, imagine that I'm sitting there in the right seat beside you, enjoying the flight with you. That's where I intend to be.

Love you forever, hon."

Carley listened to the tape several times before she finally put it on the seat beside her and drove away.

* * *

Sitting across from Dr. Copeland at her usual Wednesday session, Carley sadly related her loss, the memorial service, and the tape recording.

"I heard about the accident. I'm so sorry for your loss, Carley." Copeland said, looking at her with sad eyes.

"Thanks..., yet at times I feel I've had no loss. Some would think me crazy, but I feel Patten's presence. I talk to him sometimes. I feel him with me when I need him. If that's insane, it's okay with me. He'll always be with me!"

Copeland gazed at her with understanding and compassion, and then looked away.

"I think he will be!"

"There is another way Patten will be with me: I'm carrying his baby boy. I'll name him Steve. I think Patten would appreciate that—his son, named Steve, died at the age of fourteen. I do wish he'd known I'm pregnant with his son...

"I told Jack I'm pregnant with Patten's baby, and if he were angry with anyone it should be me; that I was lonely; that I was rejected by him; and that I sought the loving relationship I had with Patten. It has been the highlight of my life, and I think Patten's—"

"I'm sure you've been as important to him."

"I hope so…, I think so. I think it was a time in the sun, for both of us. I told Jack I didn't regret it for one instant," Carley continued, adamantly, "that Patten and I loved and needed each other, and that Jack seemed to neither love nor need anyone.

She became animated: "You know what? Jack wasn't upset! He didn't care enough about me to be jealous! Patten said to me once: 'no jealousy, no love.' He was right!

"Jack's itching to go off into the world again, so he's pleased that he can be divorced and free. Mark and I are moving to Atlanta to be near my aunt, and we'll leave in the next few days in case Katrina comes ashore around here.

"Jack's mother is going to be lonely, I'm sure, as she sees that her dream of having her son and his family live close by just won't happen. I guess for all of us in some ways life is a succession of letting go—of turning loose—of dreams, hopes, and wishes, as well as loved ones. That's painful!

"I've decided I can't always protect Mark from the fact that his father doesn't want to be tied down with a family at this time in his life. Jack has other things he wants to do, and we will go our own way." She paused for a moment. "Yet I do blame Jack for marrying me and wanting children when a family was really not important to him."

After a short silence, she spoke wistfully: "It's so sad that it took Patten's death to shock me into finally breaking down—what Patten would call—an old wall erected years ago. That wall was crumbling, but is now gone for good, and I'll be able to get on with my life."

*　*　*

Early next morning Carley flew the Cherokee one-forty along the coastline. She slowed to 65 knots, unlatched and pushed open the small access window at her shoulder. Holding the urn up to the window, she watched as the low pressure created by the rushing wind whisked the ashes out into the Gulf.

"Goodbye, my love," she whispered. Tears trickled down her cheeks as she banked left and headed toward the airport.